SLEY HOUSE PUBLISHING

Tales of Sley House 2021

First edition

ISBN: 978-1-7373102-2-8

Editing by K. A. Hough
Editing by Trevor Willliamson

This book was professionally typeset on Reedsy.
Find out more at reedsy.com

Contents

Foreword

In deciding what we wanted for our first anthology, we knew it must address the genres in which we are interested in publishing here at Sley House. By and large, I think this selection of short stories accomplishes this. We worked off a relatively short window from creation of the publishing house to announcing submissions were open, and still we received some strong stories. I wish we could have published them all.

We also knew we wanted to give a voice to students of creative writing. This will be the first of two traditions we will continue in future anthologies. Another is that our editors will work closely with authors whose stories show promise.

We hope you enjoy these stories. We hope you are drawn into Sley House and find that you never want to leave. That the walls of our home envelop you with its secrets, its treasures, and its horrors, and you are dying to see what comes next.

About the editors —

K. A. Hough –
   K.A. Hough is a Canadian writer and editor who balances her passion for exercise and science with her love of cookies and nonsense. She has a voracious appetite for reading, especially

for rediscovering the classics: everything from Austen to du Maurier and Atwood to Wilde, as well as modern humorists like Douglas Adams and David Sedaris. Her guilty pleasures are Mammy Walsh and Inspector Poirot.

She lives with her husband, three far-too-energetic kids, and a codependent dog. In her spare time, she writes stories and personal essays, teaches boot camps in the parks, and drinks tea.

Her first novel, *Ground Control*, was published by Lights Out Ink press in April 2021.

Trevor Williamson –

Trevor Williamson was born with a book in his hand and a library card in his pocket. He has fostered a lifelong love for stories and spends the majority of his time daydreaming about the many stories he reads. He currently resides in Arkansas with his wife and dog and works as a college instructor and an academic coordinator for a college athletics program. He holds a B.A. in Modern Languages with an emphasis in Spanish, and an M.A. in Spanish Literature, and has published in classical Spanish textbooks for intermediate Spanish readers, an encyclopedia of comic books, and some short fiction. He joined Sley House as an editor in 2021 and co-hosts the *Sley House Presents Lit Bits* podcast.

Preface

Houses harbor more than just our lives, shelter more than just our bodies. They harbor our darkest fears. Shelter our secrets. Sley House is no different. It has stood for generations, harboring numerous generations of the family Sley, more than just my brother and I — its current occupants. It has sheltered countless against the cold, the rain, the snow, the heat, and the sun.

My brother RG and I are old men, though he is much older than I. We each had wives once, though both have long passed on. We both have children, all are off caring for their own families now. A nurse visits us three times a week, a doctor comes once a week, and a trusted manservant and his young family look after not just our day-to-day needs, but also the needs of the house. We have invested the Sley family fortune wisely: banking and real estate mostly, but as avid learners and avid readers, we have invested in this new endeavor: this publishing house. No matter how we built our fortune, learning and literacy have always been our business.

When we first met Jeremy, Trevor, and Karen, we knew that with their combined experience, they were the right captains to steer this ship that carries our family name. We have invested conservatively, not because we don't believe in the business or in their vision, but because we have habitually built successful businesses from the ground up, incurring little to no debt. We want Sley House to last long after we are gone, and for that to happen, we are monitoring them carefully as they build this new house.

They will harbor our name in the growth of this company and will shelter all our futures and the futures of the writers who join us. We, in turn, trust them with our secrets, with our fears, and with (some of) our fortune.

And with you, dear reader, we are entrusting you with just *some* of our secrets.

Hidden away in the darkest crevices, in the deepest recesses, our secrets sleep alongside our fears, all sheltered by this house. We let them out sometimes, but never out of sight. We let them curl up at our feet by the fire in the great room. We entertain them through seances in the parlor. Feed them with rituals at the altar in the basement. Give them names we learn by reading the grimoires and spiritual books that line the shelves in our library, among the fiction and the poetry and the biographies.

Some of those secrets and fears are rational. For example, I once kissed my brother's girlfriend. We were in high school, and it was a stolen moment between us. To this day, my brother (who is too bedridden and medicated now to read this) has never found out this secret. Given my brother's weak constitution and his wasting illness, I fear the day I walk in his bedroom to find him no longer with me.

Other secrets, other fears may not be as rational. Should I tell you the names of all I've prayed to, over the years? No, I think not, as some of them do not want to be known. Should I tell you what they have threatened me with, should I reveal them? I won't divulge that, either. Do I care that you think me irrational, or worse, that you'd question my sanity? No; for, once you read the stories we've collected in this book, you'll better understand my fears — both rational and otherwise — and why I keep the secrets that I keep.

What secrets do you keep? What keeps you awake at night, dumb with fear? We'll see, in the following pages, if your fears align with the nightmares we've captured in these pages, or if your secrets are as unforgiving as some of the secrets we've exposed here. Soon enough, we'll be able to gauge the level of your madness and the depravity of your soul, and know if you are a worthy sojourner to visit Sley House. But beware, for the secrets and fears addressed in this first anthology only hint at the darkest corners of Sley House.

Welcome.

—Charles Sley

Acknowledgement

I would like to thank first our editors and the members of team Sley House: K. A. Hough and Trevor Williamson.

I would also like to thank our contributors: Matthew Anthony Allair, N. A. Battaglia, Evan Baughfman, K. D. Bowers, Arasibo Campeche, Koji A. Dae, Dale Hankins, J. D. Harlock, Curtis Harrell, Priscilla Kint, Erik McHatton, Jacob Steven Mohr, Darren Todd, and Rachel Unger.

I would also like to thank our cover artist, Milan Jovanovic, who did a phenomenal job. Our producers at Wayne Howard Studios, Les Eason and Curtis Steen, who have helped our podcast — Sley House Publishing Presents "Lit Bits" — and by extension, Trevor and me, sound professional: Thank you both for giving Sley House a voice.

To our benefactors — the Sley brothers — thank you for trusting us with this venture.

And to my wife, Kerri—thank you for your support and your strength. I love you always, my dear.

— Jeremy Billingsley

Appetite for Fear

Evan Baughfman

Merle Gunderson wondered if the dead old woman before him, Ms. Bessy Hill, had any relation whatsoever to the cadaver he'd prepared for burial a week ago. He certainly hoped not.

The previous Tuesday, Mrs. Valeria Vincent had been delivered to Merle's funeral home. On her left hand, the deceased wore a dazzling diamond ring. Merle had deftly removed the piece of jewelry and, the following morning, pawned it off at a shop two counties over.

Later, Mrs. Vincent's wiry son, Curtis, flanked by a pair of gorilla-fisted friends, had appeared at Merle's workplace, asking for the glittery family heirloom. Merle had denied ever seeing anything sparkling on the lady's fingers.

To his credit, Curtis Vincent had not been convinced, and, at his mother's service on Saturday, presented Merle with an ultimatum: return the ring or end up choking on six feet of dirt.

"Bring it back in one week," Curtis said, "looking all shiny and new. If for some reason you can't procure what's rightfully mine, I'll also accept a payment of fifty thousand dollars."

Merle didn't even have a tenth of that scratch to give. And the pawnshop had already sold Mrs. Vincent's ring within hours of Merle's visit.

So, everywhere he went, Merle had a revolver on his hip, hidden under a coat, in case Curtis Vincent came to collect early. Merle didn't exactly know how to use the weapon; though, the pawnshop's proprietor had given him a few pointers after the sale.

Now, in Merle's mortuary, beneath flickering lights, Bessy Hill reminded Merle far too much of Valeria Vincent. Both women had the same gray bob, the same pallid lips. Each had a beauty mark beside her left eye. Mrs. Vincent's mark, however, had looked decidedly more wart-like.

In other words, the ladies could have been twins. The thought of Curtis stopping by to check in on his "Aunt Bessy" curdled Merle's blood more than a werewolf's howl or the wail of a ghost. More than the prospect of thirteen ghosts!

To be fair, Merle had been working with the dead for nearly a decade and had never experienced a supernatural encounter. Because of his profession, though, he'd often witnessed the aftermath of violence between his fellow man. And if there was anything to truly be afraid of in this world, it was the brutality of human beings.

In all likelihood, Ms. Hill and Mrs. Vincent hadn't been sisters. Bessy hadn't attended Valeria's funeral, after all.

Still, the very idea of Curtis and friends materializing at Merle's doorway brought the mortician's trembling hand down to his hip. Merle listened for approaching footfalls. Fortunately, he heard nothing out of the ordinary.

Then, Bessy Hill's corpse moved atop the embalming table.

Though rigor mortis had stiffened her muscles and joints, the woman wriggled as if she were shivering from cold.

Beside the body, Merle puzzled over the unnatural shimmy. Until now, the deceased had always remained still under his care.

Two days prior, Ms. Hill had succumbed to a fatal heart attack and tumbled down her staircase, her spine snapping along unforgiving steps. Merle had spent some time straightening out the twisted spinster, preparing her for the open casket viewing her brother, Walt, had paid for.

For a brief moment, Merle expected the corpse to sit up and lunge at him in a zombified or demon-possessed state. But only the torso of "haunted" Hill quivered. The woman's eyes remained shut, unseeing. Her lips stayed sealed, unspeaking.

It soon became clear to Merle that something moved inside Bessy Hill. Something that sought escape.

But nothing bulged on the corpse's front. Merle turned the body onto its side.

Along Ms. Hill's readjusted vertebrae, a mysterious entity pushed against her skin. It looked as if the broken spine itself were trying to tear free of the woman's flesh.

"My God!" Merle backed away from the terrifying sight, leaving the body facedown on the table.

The woman's back split open. A large insect-like head emerged, antennae seemingly searching the air for Merle's presence. Massive mandibles clicked. Countless legs revealed themselves as the creature unfurled from the ragged cavity like a rising cobra.

What the hell was Merle even looking at? He'd read about giant tapeworms living inside intestines. But he'd never heard of an overgrown centipede coiled around a spinal column before!

Merle removed the revolver from its holster. He did his best to fix the gun barrel on the burgeoning bug, but his hand quaked and the sinister animal didn't exactly stay still.

Soon, the monster had climbed completely from the corpse. It was two feet long and moved for Merle, dropping to the floor.

Merle aimed the gun but quickly realized he was more likely to shoot off a toe than hit his encroaching target. "Goddamn it! No! Stop!"

He screamed as the thing came closer. Closer.

The centipede actually halted its approach and momentarily curled in on itself. It then went for Merle again.

Merle cocked the revolver's hammer. He screamed at the creature to stop. Louder. Louder!

The centipede stopped mid-stride. It curled up once more.

"You... You don't like that, do you?"

Before the bug could move another inch, Merle shrieked like a banshee. Again and again and again, keeping the creature frozen in place.

What a fascinating animal! Stunned by screams! Amazing!

Merle figured there were probably other people out there who'd find the bug of interest. Individuals willing to pay handsomely for such a curious find. So long as the specimen were still alive...

Merle holstered the revolver. He grabbed and opened a handheld organ transportation cooler.

The creature scrambled forward.

Merle screeched. The bug put on the brakes.

With a pair of forceps, Merle lifted the wriggling beast off the floor. The thing flailed in his grasp.

To calm the creature, Merle screamed full force, convincing the centipede to go limp. Next, he dropped the critter into the cooler and slammed the lid shut, locking the animal up inside its temporary prison cell.

* * *

Merle took the creature to nearby Johnston College, the institution where he'd earned his Mortuary Science degree and recently taken courses in Botany to better assist the plant life in his garden. Johnston also had an Entomology department, and that is where, inside a laboratory brightly lit by fluorescence, Merle found Dr. Rebekah Bates.

When Merle entered the lab, the doctor was dispensing crickets into a tarantula's glass enclosure. The room was stacked with terrariums housing spiders, scorpions, roaches, mantises, and other many-legged critters.

Merle shuddered in the presence of the creepy-crawly horde. Under the cooler's lid, the centipede shifted. Until that point, the creature had remained so silent that Merle thought it might've died in the dark.

Dr. Bates turned to Merle. "Yes? May I help you?"

"Hi, there," said Merle. "I've found something strange. Thought you'd be the right person to see it."

The doctor nodded to the cooler. "An insect?"

"Something like that. Ugliest damned thing I've ever had the displeasure to come across."

"Does it fly?"

"No."

"In that case..." Bates gestured to an empty terrarium at a workstation table. "Let's put it in there and have a look."

Soon, the creature was in the glass cage. It rested there, motionless.

"Incredible," said the doctor. "It resembles a *Craterostigmomorpha*. Yet…" Her mind wandered. "Where did you find this?"

Merle told the entomologist everything. She listened but never took her eyes off the multi-limbed monster.

Bates said, "A parasite, likely to have entered the host in a larval state. Do you know if the host traveled out-of-country anytime in the last year?"

"Ms. Hill?" Merle shrugged. "I never actually knew the lady until… well, you know."

Bates said, "Yes, of course. But if you could find out if she did any touristing, it might help me to determine what we're dealing with here."

"I have her brother's number back at my office."

"Excellent."

The door to the laboratory opened. A custodian entered, holding a plastic trash bag. He said, "Hey, Doc. I drew the short straw today."

"Hello, Rudy," said Bates. "Come over here for a moment?"

"You know I don't like being in here any longer than I have to be…"

The centipede came alive, wiggling its antennae.

Pointing to the creature, Bates asked, "Do you know what this is, Rudy?"

The custodian gulped and came to the cage. "Jesus! It's huge! Look at its mouth!"

Bates said, "What do you make of this carnivorous invertebrate?"

The possible *Craterostigmomorpha* was now attempting to climb the enclosure, its head peering in Rudy's direction.

"I… I…" the man stammered. He backed away from the

terrarium. "It can't... can't get out of there, right?"

"Rudy?" Bates asked again. "Care to predict what this animal might be?"

The custodian moved to a trash bin. He emptied its contents into his bag. On his way out the door, Rudy said, "That's an honest-to-goodness nightmare, is what that is."

When they were alone, Bates said to Merle, "Most people avoid this lab at all costs. They're not so good with bugs."

"I'm hardly any better," Merle replied. "I know bugs are important for the environment and all, but looking at them's never fun. Unless they're pretty, like butterflies."

"Did you notice how active this creature became when Rudy got close?"

"Yes..."

"It appears to be highly perceptive to fear. Excited by it, even. You told me it startled you when it first appeared, right? It scared you?"

"No shit, it scared me."

"It seems to target the afraid. Tell me, were you frightened of anything before it left its host?"

Merle remembered thinking of Curtis Vincent before the creature reared its hellacious head. "I was afraid of something, yeah."

"It sensed your fear," said the doctor. "Sensed it and wanted more. That's why it revealed itself to you." Bates then screamed, stopping the centipede's frenzy. She grinned. "Delightful. I don't understand why it's so susceptible to that. It'll require further study."

"Great," said Merle. "Now, how much are you willing to pay me?"

"I'm sorry? Pay you...?"

"This thing's mine. But I can let it become yours... for a price."

"I don't understand."

"Buy it from me, Doc."

"Buy it...?"

"With money! You've got some, don't you? I'm sure the college has got plenty."

"Our department's already spent its annual allocations on other things. Couldn't you donate this specimen to me, so that I may—"

"I didn't come here to give you a donation."

"Please—"

"Help me get it back in the cooler."

"I don't think that's wise. It should stay here for—"

"You're not getting this thing for free! I! Need! Money!"

"Okay, okay, just... How much?"

"Fifty grand."

"Fifty *grand*? That's ridiculous!"

"Then, I'll figure something else out! The cooler, Doc. Now!"

"No, I strongly advise against—"

Merle lifted his coat, flashing his gun. "I strongly advise against you pissing me off!"

Bates whimpered. "Don't hurt me, please. Don't..."

The creature sensed her terror. Antennae shifted the doctor's way like divining rods.

Merle shouted, "Do what I say, goddamn it! Come on!"

In that instant, power-mad Merle, staring at his very own *Craterostigmomorpha*, knew he had a potential solution to the creeping conflict with Curtis Vincent.

* * *

Thursday morning, Bessy Hill's surprisingly well-attended

service took place at Gunderson Funeral Home, outside in the aptly titled Memorial Garden. Butterflies flitted through sunshine as friends and family members shared warm stories of the dearly departed.

Younger brother Walt recounted highlights of a recent trip to South America, where he and his sister enjoyed rainforests, beaches, and foreign cuisine. Merle wondered if the old man had also brought home a parasitic entity now resting along his spine.

Days earlier, after removing Ms. Hill's kidneys, liver, and heart, Merle had stitched the woman back together. He'd then replaced her blood with embalming fluid.

Merle tried feeding her liver to his creature, but the beast ignored the treat. Unimpressed by the organ, the *Craterostigmomorpha* sat, stationary, inside its new habitat, an empty fish tank.

Merle deduced the animal preferred live prey, so he caught a rat. Unfortunately, the rodent's high-pitched squeals seemed to frighten the creature into submission, so Merle decided to feed the rat some hemlock from the garden.

Once the rat succumbed to the poison and fell into a paralytic state, Merle re-presented the rodent to his pet. The centipede no longer hesitated and fed, relishing in the tiny mammal's immense fear, savagely tearing the rat apart with lacerating mandibles.

Merle had smiled over the gory attack, imagining Curtis falling to a similar fate. Yes, he'd fashion a special concoction just for the awful Mr. Vincent.

The truth was that Merle's Memorial Garden held a dark secret: it was actually a jungle of deadly vegetation. Aside from the hemlock, the garden displayed nightshade, strychnine trees, and *Chondrodendron tomentosum*, all poisonous plants hidden in plain sight amongst violets, daisies, and roses.

As a mortician, Merle obviously had a fascination with death. And he found the plants' juxtaposition of beauty and lethality particularly captivating. He tended to his garden with great care, eager to share its eerie, natural duality with visitors to his estate.

It always tickled Merle that nobody knew they paid their respects under strychnine-laced shade. People had no clue, either, that their loved one's organs were below their feet and part of the serene scene.

For years, Merle had been extracting body parts from the corpses under his care. He'd bury them into the earth, believing his plants thrived on the discarded pieces, that they absorbed all remaining lifeforce into their roots. Merle often gifted organs to subterranean worms and beetles he'd never see. He imagined bugs venturing from far-off places just to get a taste of Ms. Hill's heart and kidneys, simultaneously tilling the soil while filling up their little bellies.

When Ms. Hill's service was over, Merle got some assistance loading her casket into his hearse. He then led the funeral procession to Elysian Castle Cemetery.

Once at E.C.C., the site's caretaker guided pallbearers along the correct path to Bessy's grave. His job done for the day, Merle closed the hearse's back hatch.

A hand gripped his shoulder. Merle turned, finding himself face-to-face with Valeria Vincent's son.

Holding a bouquet of vibrant flowers, Curtis said, "Here to see Mom. But happier to see you."

"I don't have your money or your ring."

"Yet. Yeah? 'I don't have your money or your ring *yet*.' Don't

10

sound so down, pal. You've still got time. Plenty of time. Although, fair warning: I don't eat breakfast. Just need coffee, then I'm ready to go. See you Saturday, early."

The gun at Merle's side was begging to be used. But Merle just said, "I'll be waiting."

Curtis smirked. "Wow. Am I hearing some attitude there? Not very smart. No, no, no." He gestured to tombstones. "Wise up, or I put you in a place that's nowhere near as nice as this. *Ciao*." Curtis walked away to visit his mother.

Merle glanced at his knock-off wristwatch. He had forty-three hours to finalize preparations for Curtis and friends.

Part of Merle wished the clock would tick faster. He could hardly wait to ignite some fear inside the tough guys' eyes.

* * *

On Saturday, Merle woke well before dawn. His house was directly behind the funeral home, on the other side of the Memorial Garden. In the garden, he double-checked that everything was as he'd left it the night before.

At 6:59 a.m., a rusty pickup pulled onto the property. Out stepped Curtis and his two cronies. The larger of the pair, the driver, reached into the back of the truck and retrieved a shotgun. The smaller giant already had a baseball bat in his grasp. Since Merle's nearest neighbor was a half-mile away, they probably figured they were about to have some fun.

Curtis led them to Merle, who was standing on the front lawn. Curtis wore brass knuckles on each hand. "Now, this is bold," he said. "If I were you, I would've left town a while ago."

"Why run," said Merle, "when I have what your mother lost?"

"Oh, yeah? Found it somewhere, did you?"

"Much easier to find than fifty grand, that's for sure."

Curtis exchanged looks with his friends. "And here we were

11

hoping for a payday."

"Don't worry," said Merle. "You'll get what's yours. Come with me, to the garden."

Curtis didn't move. "The garden? Why?"

"I know you're still planning on teaching me a lesson. So, if you're going to kick my ass anyway, why not at least let me choose where it happens?"

Curtis shrugged. "I think we can accommodate that."

Boob Ruth and Driver chuckled.

"Thank you," said Merle. The trio followed him through the grass, to the garden.

Driver was the first to scream. A long syringe had gone through the flimsy sole of his weathered tennis shoe, its needle embedded in the bottom of his foot. The man dropped the shotgun and, cursing, hopped around like a wounded jackrabbit. Soon, he stepped on a second syringe. His other foot now in pain, Driver collapsed, falling upon a few more well-positioned needles, squealing like a stuck pig.

It took a few moments for Curtis and his remaining companion to realize that they had walked into a trap. By the time they turned to Merle, the mortician had his revolver ready. He fired a round directly into Boob Ruth's chest. The wannabe ballplayer fell into his own nest of needles.

The previous day, Merle had meticulously concealed four dozen syringes around the garden. They had been filled with either embalming fluid or hemlock extract. A few even contained a mixture of both.

Merle had also spent the past few days doing target practice on bottles and cans. Dropping Boob Ruth from six feet away had been the easiest shot he'd made all week.

Bug-eyed, Curtis watched his friends suffer in the grass. He said to Merle, "I... I get it, okay? Let me leave, and I won't... won't bother you anymore."

Merle shook his head. With the gun, he indicated to nearby syringes. "Choose one. Pick it up."

"But—"

"Choose one!"

With a shaky palm, Curtis plucked a syringe from the earth. Inside the glass vial, yellow liquid shone.

"Embalming fluid," Merle explained. "Jab it into your thigh."

"What—"

Merle shot a bullet over Curtis's head. "Do as I say!"

Curtis wept as he injected embalming fluid into his leg. "God... please..."

Beside him, his fallen comrades had gone silent and still. Boob Ruth appeared to be dead, and the hemlock had already parked Driver into paralysis.

"That was fun, but grab another one," Merle demanded. "Make sure its contents look clear."

Curtis complied. When told to do so, he plunged hemlock into his own neck with little hesitation. Soon, Curtis lay sprawled in the garden, as useless as his friends.

Merle left for a moment and returned with a handheld cooler. He said, "You can't move, can you? But you can think. You can *fear*." Merle giggled. "You know, I was going to toy with you a bit, and make up some nonsense about having your mother's heart in here. I was going to tell you that I kept her heart as my own personal trophy. But things have escalated rather quickly, haven't they? So, why not keep up the current pace and just get on with the main attraction already?"

Merle lifted the cooler lid and dumped his creature onto Curtis's sternum. The *Craterostigmomorpha* went for the man's quiet throat and began to feast.

Merle grinned. "I call this thing a 'fear-eater'. Thanks for giving it plenty to chew on."

After watching the carnage for a few minutes, Merle walked off to retrieve a bone saw and shovel. When he returned, Curtis's face was completely gone. The man's eyeless skull stared up at Merle with a toothy grimace.

The fear-eater had now crawled over to the paralyzed Driver, peeling away the brute's cheeks and lips, gorging itself on the guy's tongue.

Soon thereafter, the fear-eater stopped feeding. Driver was dead, no longer afraid, and no longer on the menu.

"What a mess," said Merle.

Dismembering and burying the three corpses would certainly drain him. But it needed to be done and would ultimately be worth it in the end. The extra meat would definitely fortify his flora.

Before getting to work, Merle made sure to take a few moments to appreciate the garden. The butterflies. The colors. The shade. He closed his eyes, basking in a pleasant breeze.

When he turned back to the bodies, the fear-eater had disappeared.

Had it scurried off into the foliage, on the search for some shivering squirrel?

Merle couldn't find the creature anywhere. He even called out for it. Of course, that yielded no results. The monster wasn't a dog.

Merle sighed and then did what he'd set out to do. He sawed each of the dead men apart. Next, he dug a series of holes and gave the various pieces and appendages to the earth.

Through it all, Merle hoped the fear-eater would come back

to him. It never did.

Exhausted, the mortician, filthy and achy, trudged back home for a shower and a nap. He decided to put off cleaning the syringe minefield until the afternoon.

* * *

Merle overslept, awaking seven hours later. Once back in the garden, he began to place needles into a metal pail. That's when he noticed something odd hanging from his hemlock.

At first, Merle didn't understand what he was looking at. Then it became clear: the fear-eater had built itself—and entered into—an enormous cocoon. Merle could see a faint outline of the creature inside the semi-transparent structure.

Stunned, Merle said, "You beautiful bastard…"

The fear-eater wasn't a *Craterostigmomorpha*, after all. Not a centipede.

No, it was some kind of killer caterpillar. A pernicious pupa.

And it would soon morph into its final form, a flying nightmare.

A big, bad butterfly? A murderous, mutant moth?

How long until the monster changed? How long until it took flight?

Merle ran into his house and phoned the Johnston College Entomology Department. It was late on a Saturday, and near sundown, but maybe Dr. Bates was pulling a weekend shift. Someone had to make sure the bugs stayed fed, right?

After the third ring, a voice said, "Hello, this is Dr. Bates."

"Thank God!"

"Who is this?"

"Merle Gunderson. You remember me, yeah?"

Silence for a few seconds. Then: "Don't ever call here again." The doctor hung up.

15

Merle called again. Bates didn't answer this time. Merle left a message in her voicemail, detailing his latest discovery. He gave her his number and waited for her to contact him.

It only took two minutes until the doctor was on the other line, asking, "Is this a prank, Mr. Gunderson? I'd really appreciate you not harassing me with nonsense."

"No nonsense!" Merle said. "A no-bullshit cocoon! A huge one! How long, you think, until the thing hatches?"

"For most moth and butterfly species, it takes anywhere from five to twenty days for the insect to emerge from its cocoon or chrysalis."

"Okay. So, I've got plenty of time, then?"

"I honestly have no idea. This animal is unlike anything I've encountered before."

"I think the thing's maybe from Brazil or… or Peru…"

"That doesn't really help me, at the moment. I'd like to see the cocoon up close, in person."

"Well, actually… I don't know if that's such a good idea."

Syringes were still stuck in the ground, and blood still stained the grass.

Bates said, "You called me, yes? I heard panic and urgency in your voice, or did I not?"

"I… I just wanted information… your opinion… advice."

"My advice is that I come over and take a look at what's in your garden as soon as possible."

"You don't have to, really."

"Honestly, I was trying to forget that I'd ever met you, but you've pulled me right back into this. That animal, once it completes metamorphosis, could be extremely dangerous. I need to take the most responsible course of action here."

"Look, I'm sorry that I called," said Merle.

16

"No, I think you made the right decision. I'll be on my way soon."

"No, no. I don't want you here!"

"I think I have to be."

"Just... Just stay away! You aren't welcome on my property. I don't want to, but if you come, I'll... I'll..."

"I don't think you'll be threatening me with a gun this time around."

"No? What makes you so sure about that?"

"Because I'll have the police escorting me as I arrive!" The doctor hung up again.

Merle screamed at his phone and threw it against the wall.

Now the authorities were getting involved? The last thing Merle needed was for cops to come out to his crime scene! How could he have been so careless with that phone call? So desperate? So dumb?

"Stupid, stupid, *stupid!*" Merle smacked himself upside the head before racing back to the garden.

He had to dispose of the syringes. He had to hose the grass clean. He had to do a far more convincing job of smoothing out the areas where he'd buried Curtis and company.

But hosing the dried blood didn't make the gore disappear. It only gave the grass a suspiciously rosy complexion. Maybe Merle had to mow away the massacre?

Yeah, yeah! That might do the trick!

Careful not to prick himself, Merle collected syringes, dropping them into the pail. After that, he sprinted to the toolshed, pulling out a lawnmower.

At the garden, he yanked on the mower's starter cord. The machine refused to rumble. He yanked the cord twice more. Again. Again. Again.

Merle shrieked. "Come on! Come on, come on, *come on*!"

The mower did not cooperate. Merle cursed it. Kicked it. Continued to try to bring it to life.

Finally, Merle ended his efforts. He was on the verge of tears. Who knew how quickly the police would get there? How soon until they had him in handcuffs?

Merle felt frantic. Helpless. Hopeless.

Afraid.

Beside him, the cocoon peeled apart. A winged terror emerged.

"Jesus Christ!" Merle wailed. "No!"

The fear-eater had evolved into a moth-like beast. A monster with a six-foot wingspan and a razor-sharp proboscis.

Its most petrifying feature: the massive stinger at the end of its abdomen.

The animal circled above Merle, studying him. For the time being, the mortician's screams appeared to give the creature pause.

Before his shower earlier, Merle had returned his revolver to a bedroom drawer. Though, he wasn't exactly defenseless. Boob Ruth's baseball bat still lied nearby, as did Merle's bone saw and Driver's shotgun. The shovel was close, as well.

Merle's voice cracked. His screams became hoarse.

Not knowing how to work a shotgun, he dived for the bat.

The fear-eater dived for him.

Merle grabbed and gripped his weapon... and felt an awful sting between his shoulder blades.

Merle moaned and dropped to his knees. The fear-eater clamped onto his back, filling his flesh with venom.

Was it hemlock? Is that what was coursing through Merle's veins? Had the creature somehow absorbed the poison after eating the victims Merle prepared for it? Or had the cocoon's attachment to the hemlock plant somehow affected the animal's physiology?

Thinking about this, Merle collapsed face-first into the grass. He'd already lost the ability to move and speak. The only screaming he did now was inside his mind.

Paralyzed, all Merle could do was distress over the inevitable: the immeasurable pain and certain death coming his way.

The fear-eater lanced its proboscis through Merle's skull and sucked the terror straight from his brain.

Some time later, police sirens approached. As the sound grew louder and shriller, the monster became more and more agitated.

It eventually sprang from Merle's body, carrying the dead man's head along with it, up into the darkening sky.

Solver

Darren Todd

S
o I got a call from the sheriff's office about my nine-year-old son, Tilly. Not the best cap to an otherwise productive morning. I asked why, but they just said to come into the school A-SAP. For me, that meant about twelve minutes—the time it took me to throw on slacks (I was still in PJs, working remote) and head out the door.

Off I went, pretty much only the worst scenarios zipping through my brain. I reached the school and half-jogged into the principal's office. I found Tilly seated beside the secretary, and most of my worry dissolved just seeing him there, unhurt. Before I could even offer a greeting or ask him what all this was about, the voice from the phone came from my right. "Mr. Solver." A sheriff's deputy. "This way, please."

Now, I hadn't been an apple polisher in school, but I was no riff-raff, either. And yet, when that deputy summoned me into the principal's office and I entered to find the sheriff and Tilly's homeroom teacher also sitting in there waiting for me, I felt like I was Tilly's age again, busted for cutting up in Ms. Clendenon's class. And everyone knew that the *principal's* paddle was way worse that any teacher's.

20

But that was a long time ago. While my principal was an aloof older man, Tilly's principal had always come across as an approachable, even funny lady and not ten years my senior. Had a poster on her office wall reading: "Remember: the principal is a pal."

But not that day. That morning, her face looked dour, sullen even, like she was second guessing a career in education. The sheriff pointed to a table against the far wall. "Mr. Solver. Can I have you take a look at this?" Not a request. I followed his finger, walked over to the table, leaned down to inspect the item. It didn't take long. Sure enough, it was Tilly's handiwork, and yeah, he was probably in real trouble.

Cut to two months prior—beginning of school, fourth grade. Familiar faces interspersed with a few new ones. Tilly was fine—not happy to see the end of summer break, but fine. Problem was, I couldn't get that kid to do much. His mom and I had always shared the belief that school should be a kid's only job, and I've tried my best to carry that over since she's been gone. But Tilly would come home supposedly tapped out and want to do nothing but watch TV or stare at his tablet till bedtime. I tried STEM projects, a "hands-on sensory science kit," even LEGOs—nothing clicked.

"I'm bored. What do you expect me to do?" he'd ask me.

"You're a Solver," I'd tell him. "Figure it out."

He'd play when I made him, and he had his share of outside time with the kids in our condo complex, but as far as anything approaching a hobby, I was stumped.

Then I saw this ad on Facebook. You know the type: you just think about taking a Caribbean cruise and suddenly that's the only ad you see—like Zuckerberg is peering into your soul. I saw a kid Tilly's age playing with action figures, but then it said that the kid made them himself. He made the vehicles, the fort, all of it. Showed the kid microwaving these plastic pellets, mixing in some color, and crafting a stand for his tablet, a toothbrush holder, a little—what do you call those things on the end of fabric ties?—*those*, so that the drawstrings on his shorts didn't retreat into the waistband.

Melty Makes they called them. Low-melting point, moldable plastic, and I was sold.

So was Tilly. When they came in the mail, I worried for a minute that they'd join the ranks of the other failed creative experiments, so I waited till the weekend—a Saturday morning—and I started making my own widget, a grip for a slim pencil. Something I hadn't even seen since grade school, but innocuous enough and easy to make. Even added some blue pellets for flare. Sure enough…

"Whatcha making, Dad?" He moseyed into the kitchen, curious.

"Eh, just messing around with this stuff I found online. For crafting your own tools or… whatever."

"Can I try?"

"Well, it's not really a toy, though I guess you could make toys out of it. Sure, why not?"

A little psychological nudge never hurt anybody, and that did it. Next thing I knew, the whole condo was fair game. Broken lid: "I'll make one." Complete with threading and sanded smooth. Tape dispenser holds the roll all crooked: "Got it." Lost the back to the universal remote: "I'm on it." And he'd grab some Melty Makes, his little cauldron dish, and then it was the ding of the microwave over and over till he got it just right.

The Melty Makes come in this cylinder—reminds me of a

mini time capsule. One tube is, like, fifteen bucks, but I couldn't complain; I'd struck creative gold. Soon, I was telling him to take breaks and *watch* tv.

Didn't take long for this to seep into his school life. By this time, he'd made his own Pokémon necklaces and figurines (trademark be damned). He'd made these amazing little fingers for the Wicked Witch of the East for *The Wizard of Oz* play; was selling—regularly—these custom little army guys, all colors and full of detail. A teacher even bought some for a classroom reenactment diorama. Tilly was paying for his own Melty Makes before long and still had money left over for a new deck of Pokémon cards every Monday after school.

Till one Monday. He seemed lost in thought in the back seat, but no worries. School was going great, but he still had his off days, same as any other kid, any *person*. He didn't notice when we pulled into Atomic Comics, so I cut off the car and turned back toward him. "Something banging around in there?"

He kinda jumped, shook his head.

"You gonna get your cards? I'll send you in alone if that's all right. Gotta text Uncle Vince back."

He said: "I'm not getting anything today."

"Oh, I can go in with you. It's fine. I just—"

"It's not that," he told me. "I don't have any money."

"Sure you do. You've gone to school with a ton of stuff lately. You didn't blow it all on a bunch of candy, or—"

"No."

"Then what?"

He said, "Forget it. I don't have money. I don't want any cards anyway. They're dumb. I just wanna go home."

Dadding 101: Even if it's obvious something's wrong, you pick your battles. Sometimes things work themselves out.

"All right, bud. Home then."

But this one didn't work itself out. Not that day. Not the day after when he obviously took a box of his best Pokémon cards to school, and they never made it home. And not over the following weeks, while I watched my bright, engaged, happy kid turn into a wilting flower, a dying bug curling in on itself as if to take up as little space as possible.

No more Melty Makes. One container still had a few pellets inside, enough for—well, something. I found it chucked into the trash.

An assumption many non-parents make is that sad, lonely, angry kids just need a parent to break the spell. "If only that kid's dad or mom had paid attention, they could have stepped in and kept it from happening." Whatever ugly eventuality "it" represents.

And every parent—at least any around their kid on a daily basis—knows that this is complete crap. I saw what was happening. I found a way of asking about it—no judgment or punishment—every day. And also every day, I hit wall after wall.

Indulge me an odd sidebar. Back when Tilly's mom was alive—hell, before Tilly was even conceived—we watched *300* in theaters. The brave Spartans, remember? Sure, it included some of the darker components of Spartan society. The infanticide of children born with deformities. Kids no older than Tilly being taken from their parents for training. Spartans only had one job, if you recall. But the result looked great on screen: a sea of enslaved soldiers, charlatan mystics, unscrupulous mercs, all dashed against the shield and skewered on the spear of free Spartans. A society with no interest in the yoke, no concern for whatever the rest of the world—soft and flawed—thought of their warrior ways.

Years later, even with the Spartan helmet still gracing the bumpers of "no pain, no gain" athletes, I learned the truth. Sparta was not free. First off, they had plenty of slaves. And even their people allowed to live past infancy and who'd trained from early boyhood to manhood weren't free. Free from slavery, perhaps, but not from bullies. In that society, infighting was not only allowed, it was encouraged. Sink or swim. Fight or die. Or don't die; just wilt and carry on.

At the end of the film, we get one more feel-good moment when the sole survivor of Thermopylae leads a more even battle against Xerxes' forces—the victory assured. What they didn't show was that warrior cultures unconcerned with the "lesser" members of their citizenry: the creative, the compassionate, the visionaries—they all lose in the end. Innovation has claimed far more victories than some glorified peer pressure.

Noble French knights at the Battle of Agincourt, facing a rain of arrows from decidedly *ig*noble English longbowmen. The mighty Aztecs, fierce warriors armed with obsidian swords, found that Spanish bullets made short work of all their training and ferocity. The Ottomans using cannons to introduce walled-off Constantinople to the wonders of fast-flying lead.

Bullies eventually lose to smarter people. To innovators, craftsmen, to ingenuity, overcoming any brute-force advantage.

So, looking over that table in the principal's office, down at the two-tone, beautifully crafted, ornate, and rather magnificent push-handle *shiv* bearing the telltale matte finish of a Melty Makes creation, I knew what had happened before the sheriff filled me in.

25

"It seems your son used that weapon on a fellow student."

Jeb Bishop, I thought but did not say.

"Is he all right?" I asked. "The student." I looked to the principal.

"He is. But he'll be spending the night at Mayford Memorial because of what happened."

I could have mentioned that fateful day when Tilly finally told me what was going on, when I learned the name and nature of his tormentor, but why?

"What will this mean for Tilly?" I asked. "I mean, surely this was some sort of accident."

"We're taking Tilly's excellent record into account here," the principal said, steepling her fingers. "But some of the other students mentioned a... history between Tilly and Mr. Bishop."

The sheriff asked, "Is that something you're aware of, Mr. Solver? Did your son talk to you about this... dust up?"

Dust up. Hmm. A kind way of referring to Tilly's interactions with that little bastard, Jeb. In the pregnant pause following the sheriff's question, I thought back just a few days to catching an odd stench between the kitchen and the dining room. That's where we keep the trash, and despite the lid, it can get pretty ripe, especially with just two bachelors using it and only making it to the dumpster once a week or so.

But no; that wasn't it. I followed my nose, pacing, and Tilly saw me. "Something stinks," I told him. Before, he'd have laughed about it, but now not only didn't he laugh, he looked worried. I kept searching and zeroed in on his school backpack, but when I picked it up, he launched from the couch and yanked it away from me.

"Whoa! What's going on?" I asked him.

"Nothing."

That was all I ever got.

"It's nothing." He said again.

Best and worst part of being a single parent: You can always pull rank even if you pay for it later in resentment and lost trust and silent treatment. But it had gone on too long.

"Give me the backpack right now."

I saw the resentment, of course, but the relief as well.

The smell crescendoed as I took the pack over to the table and opened it up. The acrid stench of something old and sullied wafted out, like ammonia with a carrion kicker.

This wasn't spoiled lunch he'd forgotten to take out or a shirt he'd muddied and left in there. I pulled out a couple of books, a folder, his empty water bottle. At the bottom, the familiar shape of a Melty Makes container. I reached for it, but registered something… off right away. First the weight of it, teetering, but no rattle of the plastic balls obeying gravity. It felt damp, too.

I pulled it free from the pack, into the light, and saw the pellets floating in a yellow liquid. My brain connected the color, the smell, even Tilly's dour expression, progressing to near agony now, and it all came clear.

"Is this piss? Pee?" I asked. Before he could make a sound, I said, "Whose pee is it?" 'Cause it sure as hell wasn't his.

"Jeb Bishop," Tilly said, an invisible weight settling on his shoulders at just speaking the name. "He said I have to carry it around."

"Why?" I demanded, my blood hot, teeth clenched.

Tilly kept his head down. "I paid him, but I ran out of money. It wasn't enough."

"And it never will be."

This seemed to stagger Tilly, who pulled back. I don't know

what he expected from coming clean about the bullying, but clearly my reaction surprised him.

"So there's nothing I can do." His voice cracked, tears pending.

I opened the trash can and dropped the container of bully piss inside. A moment later, I folded up the backpack and put it in the receptacle as well.

Right here, I faced several available roads. One was to act the diplomat: inform the school and insist that we have a conference with the kid and his parents. Second road: I give Tilly the wizened mentor speech about how bullies only speak one language and it was time to hit the weights, punch some leather, and cue the training montage.

And then there was option C. I opened the hall closet, reached past the blankets and pillows, and pulled out a fresh tube of Melty Makes. Of course I had a spare. I had spare batteries, spare Nerf darts, spare swimming goggles. You can bet I had a spare tube of the stuff that had awakened my son's curiosity, that he'd used to express himself, to form a foundation of work ethic, to... solve problems.

I put the tube in his hands and pulled his chin—wet with tears—up so his eyes met mine. "You're a Solver, Tilly. Same as me. Same as my father and his father before him. So there is something you can do." I tapped the cylinder of Melty Makes. "You can solve the problem."

Now, back in the stuffy confines of the principal's office, I realized they were all looking at me. I cocked my head and raised my eyebrows.

The sheriff coughed. "I said, did you know about this?"

Then it occurred to me: They were hoping for a confession. Looking to assign blame. If Tilly had just shanked this

28

punk—open, shut—there'd be no discussion. He'd be expelled, and he'd have a behavioral stain on his record that would follow him to the next school and maybe the one after that. Zero tolerance.

No one was looking for a leaky jar of urine that my son had to carry around like some stinking, shameful totem. No one asking Jeb Bishop's folks how their kid managed to tyrannize his class with impunity. They needed a confession because they had nothing. The kids had given them nothing.

I looked down at the knife again. Beautiful, really. His best work. And I had to fight to keep a smile from curling up the corners of my mouth.

I turned to the sheriff, eyebrows up, frown in place, shoulders slumped. "I never knew about any of this. But it must have been an accident. This... *thing*, has got to be an art project or something, right? The boys were just playing around, surely. This is Tilly we're talking about. You can't think...."

I let the idea linger.

A tacit consensus suffused the room. Eye contact tennis matches that ended in the principal's court.

"The boys said it was an accident. That they were goofing off." Her eyes turned to the knife. "But we can't have anything like a weapon on school grounds, Mr. Solver. Art project or not."

"Of course."

She sighed. "It's only a coupla days till fall break. Tilly will be suspended those two days, but return after the break." She held up a finger. "Though under a strict probation. Such behavior—"

"I understand," I told her, all of them. "And thank you. He'll be no more trouble."

As I left with Tilly, somber expression firmly in place, I thought of Jeb Bishop, a handful of miles away, lying in an inpatient bed at Mayford Memorial, parent beside him... or maybe left to stew in his thoughts, the throb of his wound still shooting arcs up his spine despite the meds. Claiming it had all been an accident. Going along with that story. Out of what? Fear? Respect? I didn't care.

I thought about all the bullies out there, wondering whether tomorrow would be the day when their brute strength would fail, when ingenuity and artifice would topple their primitive tyranny like a despot's statue following a rebellion.

Tilly would suffer no punishment from me for breaking his chains. *He* was not in trouble.

They were.

The Collection

Priscilla Kint

I wasn't a stranger to making bad decisions, but this one took the crown. I could hear my brother's voice in my head. *Salina, have you lost your marbles?* I'd heard the stories, knew of the myths and the legends and the old sailors who came back to shore and told their tales of how they'd survived — *they'd survived* — but only barely. Only because they'd been wise. Only because of the wax in their ears or a will as strong as iron.

But no. I'd invited a Siren on board of *The Belle-Fleur* anyway.

The ship moved around me, the steady rise and fall of the waves second nature to me by now. I was in the hull, below the quarterdeck, sitting with my head in my hands and my elbows on my knees. The wood around me creaked as the rain fell on the deck above. Occasionally, people walked this way and that, carrying lengths of rope or crates of ale we'd taken from the mainland.

Everyone was doing their part to keep the ship going and maintain our wellbeing — and I'd somehow managed to attract a monster.

I breathed in the salty air. My brown hair fell down my face in greasy strands.

Sirens were dangerous. Everyone knew that. They ensnared men with their beautiful voices and lured them under the surface, only to rake them up and feast on their flesh. They were bad news.

At least eighty percent of our crew was male, so, while the Siren might not be able to get to me, it had plenty of victims to choose from. Too many for her to be allowed to roam *The Belle-Fleur* freely.

So I needed to clean up my mess. I had to go back to my cabin, kick her off the ship, and make sure she wouldn't come back. Three simple steps. I could do that.

I stood up, ready to march to the Siren and give her a piece of my mind — but then Tommy and Azo came round the corner. Azo, our boatswain, had dark, thick eyebrows and a bald head he usually covered with a tricorn hat. Today, however, it was gleaming proudly.

Tommy, who could generally be found cleaning the deck, looked at me, his brown eyes wide. "Hey, Salina, what are you doing?"

I shook my head, hoping I didn't look as guilty as I felt. "Nothing. Just... thinking."

"Careful," Azo smirked. "You might hurt yourself."

"Shouldn't you be watching the sails?" I asked.

"We do get breaks sometimes." He looked me up and down, then stared at the crate I'd been sitting on. "I'm sure you know all about those."

I chewed the inside of my lip.

"Well, if you're not busy..." Tommy began. "Could you help me move the pork? We may have a rat problem."

"Sure," I said. We really, really couldn't use rats on board.

Especially not near our salted meat. "I'll be right with you, okay? I just need to—"

A loud crack of thunder sounded in the skies above.

"Right." I tried to gather myself. There was no way I was going to tell these two men about the Siren hiding in my cabin. So I turned to Tommy and cleared my throat. "Rats are very smart. They probably won't fall for the same traps you used last time."

"Your brother taught you that, did he?" Azo grunted.

Tommy jabbed an elbow in his ribs. Azo didn't even look like he noticed, but I did — and the message was clear. It was the same old shit, really.

The people on this ship talked behind my back a lot, but I had good ears. I knew what they thought of me. How they found it pathetic that this *girl* was running after her big brother, chasing him across the great seas. How they'd be embarrassed if it was their own sister who trailed after them like that. How I wasn't equipped to handle this life, the toughness of it.

They had it all completely wrong, of course. Elio was the younger of the two of us. He wasn't a heroic oldest brother going off on a quest. No, he was in over his head, and I was supposed to save him from guaranteed disappointment. Not that that was any of the crew's business.

Most of the time, I didn't care about the rumours and the silent judgement. I loved the ocean, the feeling of the breeze through my hair as I stood at the edge of the deck, arms wide like the figurehead at the front. Still, sometimes I wanted to punch a guy. Like Azo. Right now.

"Anyway," Tommy said. His yellow toothed smile was sincere, at least. "Meet you in storage in a minute?"

"Deal."

33

There was another crack of thunder as Azo and Tommy continued to the middle of the ship, in the direction of the supplies.

I let out a long breath, checked whether I was truly alone this time, and made my way to my chambers.

I say *my* chambers, but really, it was a shared facility. Which was a problem, because there was a Siren sitting in the wooden tub in the middle of the cabin.

The monster looked up the moment I came in. "Oh, there you are! You took your sweet time."

I took the candle from its hanger in the corner and set it down beside the tub. "Time to leave."

The Siren flinched, its long legs disappearing under the water, which sloshed and splattered over the edge.

"Where are we going?" the Siren said, blinking at me with its strange, overflowing eyes.

"*You*," I emphasized, "are going back to the ocean. You're going to go your merry way and forget about our ship."

"But why?" she asked, rolling around in her tub and letting her elbows fold over the edge.

It, I tried to remind myself. *Not she, it. It's a monster.*

"Because I say so." I planted my fists in my sides, feeling the rough cotton of my shirt on the skin of my dry knuckles. It stung.

Her head turned as she considered this, lips puckered, her braided and tangled hair rolling over her shoulders. "Because you said so..." she began. It sounded like she was about to say more, but she never did.

I pushed aside someone's bedroll — Aïsha's, I thought — and planted my foot on the bare floor underneath. "Let's go."

"Right now? But I was having such a wonderful time."

34

"Yes. You can't stay. It's too dangerous. The men..." I shook my head. "And, anyway, shouldn't you go back to the water? Isn't the sea, like, your home?"

"Is it?" When she looked up at me, the temperature in the room rose. It was always a bit unnerving when someone did that — look at you as if they were expecting something from you. It wasn't like I had anything to give. Nothing that'd be worth anything to her, anyway.

She had beauty. She had men lining up for her wherever she went — I was about the most useless person she could've come across. And yet she was smiling at me as if I'd given her the world simply by allowing her on board. It made me wonder...

I stepped closer to the tub.

"I..." I was pretty sure she'd asked me a question, but I couldn't remember it.

"Come on, beautiful," she said in a voice like velvet. Her long, slender fingers stretched out to touch my cheek. I closed my eyes, allowing myself to feel her touch — nothing but her touch — for a moment. This was the most restful I'd felt since I'd left home. "I'd like to stay here just a little bit longer."

There was something I should've remembered. Something about Tommy and the ship and singing. But right now, here was this gorgeous girl with a smile like a flash of sunshine and a touch that felt like finding a hidden treasure, and whatever it was I was forgetting, it couldn't be *that* important, could it?

"Okay," I said, the word soaring out of my mouth on an exhale.

"Great!" She perked up, the water sloshing around her. Then she stepped out of the tub — naked save for a small seaweed pouch at her hip — and sat down. Water dripped off of her in steady streams, forming a puddle around her. I followed a drop that trailed from her hairline down her temple and the side of her face. It rolled over the curve of her chin, down her throat and her collarbone until—

"Wait," I said, shaking my head. "Don't you need to be inside the tub?"

She shrugged, one corner of her mouth pulling upwards. "I'm a Siren, not a fish."

"Oh." So much for my heroic attempt to give her a temporary living space by hauling buckets of seawater into our communal tub. My fingers were still sore from all the weight I'd carried up and down the steps.

"I appreciate the effort, though." She winked at me. "You're very determined. Is that why you chose life at sea? Because you knew it would be a challenge for a human like yourself?"

The word *human* drifted in and out of my mind. Human, like me. Because she was different. This creature in front of me was a Siren. "It's — it's been a challenge, yes." I swallowed, the sound loud to my own ears. "I never really chose life at sea. I needed to… I've been following my brother."

"Your brother?" She sat with her back perfectly straight, leaning on one arm, her head tilted to the side.

"Yes." I felt awkward, standing next to the tub with my hands folded behind my back.

She grabbed a sheet from Aïsha's bedroll and laid it out before her. Then she opened the pouch at her hip and rummaged inside. She took out a white shell the size of my palm, placing it in the middle of the sheet. It was wet, dripping like her hair. More shells appeared from her pouch. Scallops. Conches. Big and small, one no bigger than my fingernail. She placed them around the big one in a sort of pattern, like a spider's web. "Where's your brother headed?"

"Across the ocean. To our mother."

"Are you both going to see your mother?" she asked, eyes still on the sheet and the shells.

"I'm not." I shrugged. "Our mother left us a long time ago. We were a small family with a big debt. It was hard, but she was our mother, you know. She should've been able to handle it. But she was tired of her life. She took her most expensive tartan dresses with her, and left us, sailed away on some ship. We haven't heard from her since. Elio is determined to find her, to bring her back to us, but I know he's going to be disappointed. He's always so confident, but..." I shook my head. "She'd been drinking. A lot. Elio doesn't remember, but... She's too far gone. In every way. She doesn't care. And even if she does, I know her — she'll feel too guilty and ashamed to ever try again. She's a coward."

My words flowed out like water. All the while, the Siren was working on her sea art with relics from a faraway world.

"She sounds very different from you," she said. "I'm sorry you and your brother struggled so much." Then she looked up at me, her chest rising and falling with her breath. It was quite wondrous, how she was able to do both, breathe air and water, not bothered by one nor the other. I wished I was that capable of accepting change.

"It's fine, really. I just have to get to Elio and make sure he's okay."

"I'm sure you'll find him." She pulled the threads of her pouch to close it. "Family must be nice to have."

"You don't have a family of your own?" I asked. My heart ached as she shook her head.

"Haven't for a long time," she whispered. "It's a bit lonely, but I try to find company when I can." She smiled at me, and her eyes shimmered with something I recognised as sadness — or perhaps it was loneliness, or kindness, or…

"W-what are those?" I pointed down at the shells. Anything to stop her from noticing the growing blush on my cheeks. She'd created a huge web, with just one empty spot left next to the big white shell.

"Aren't they pretty?" she said. She took a final conch from the tangles of her hair, scraped off some green moss, and put it in place. "I like a complete collection. It's just so… satisfying. Don't you think?"

I nodded, shifted my gaze from the collection to her, and froze. She was mesmerizing, even without singing. It was in her beautiful sea green eyes.

I'd often heard people — mostly men — talk about their conquests. They'd swear that their women had the most gorgeous eyes, like the rich colours of the ocean. But that all had to be bullshit, because I had never, ever seen eyes like hers before. They didn't just have the colour of the ocean, it was as if the sea was trapped inside of them, as if her eyes were diamonds that'd managed to capture the wild water, the waves rolling through them even now.

"Yes. Very… Very pretty."

She smiled, and the room brightened. "So, what is the plan?"

"What plan?"

She was so close, but not close enough. It felt like there were these strings attached between me and her, and they were just too short to reach, pulling at me to take another step, to feel the perfect, unblemished skin of her arm.

She nodded. "Your plan to get rid of me?"

"I— I never meant to get rid of you." There was a tug in the back of my mind, a treasure of a thought that felt important, but was empty when I opened the lid.

"Oh, I must've imagined that, then."

"No, no!" I took that step closer and sat down by her side, feeling awful. Because it sounded like I blamed her when this was definitely all my fault. "I did say you had to go earlier but now… I mean you can go wherever you please, right? Nobody can tell you… can tell you…"

She sat up on her knees, towering over me. I looked up at her, at the lines of her neck and the subtle green glow that came with her scales. They were only visible in a certain light, those scales. Only in perfectly placed patches. On her cheeks. By her collarbones. On the backs of her hands. But then she'd move, and they'd be gone again. Nothing but perfect, healthy skin that glowed like moonlight.

"You were saying?" she said, and her breath landed on my lips. The scales were on her nose, too.

I wondered what her skin would feel like. Would the scales be rough underneath my fingertips? Would they feel that sticky kind of soft that fish felt when they were just out of the water? Would it feel different from my own skin at all?

The cabin was hot — burning up. "Can I touch you?" I asked, breathless. I couldn't believe I'd said the words out loud — didn't think I had, for a moment — but then she smiled, and batted her eyes. And then she kissed me.

I let her. I let my thoughts go wild and trailed after them with my hands.

Her scales smelled like seaweed and tasted like salt.

**

The next thing I knew, I was standing outside the cabin with my heart hammering in my chest and the corners of my mouth aching from smiling so much. I'd kissed her. *I'd kissed a Siren.*

And she was beautiful, and gentle, and caring.

I laughed. A single, hollow *ha!* that bounced off the ship's wooden beams and came right back to me. I'd done something no seaman had ever done before. I'd been with a Siren and walked away unscathed. I'd come close without becoming a pawn in some sick game. Because she was different, and I was different. Men were weak, but we'd been equals.

The minutes (or had it been hours?) in that cabin were a happy blur, but one thing stood out to me clearly, one promise that she'd made. She'd leave tonight. Once the deck wasn't as crowded and Azo and Tommy and the rest of the crew wouldn't stand in our way, I'd let the Siren go. No harm done to anyone, just a quiet departure after an unexpected afternoon. We'd take this day and turn it into a memory.

Once I found Elio, I'd tell him all about this girl from the sea who may be a monster, but who left when I'd asked her to. Perhaps that'd prove once and for all that having a woman on your ship wasn't a curse, but a blessing.

I spent the rest of the day in a happy daze. As if the weather was tuned into my mood, the storm eased and the sun came out. I didn't mind when Tommy put me on rat duty — as if whacking these animals with the end of a mop would help anything. I ate little, since my stomach was still as full as my head. I relayed a message to our captain from the navigator, about the course we were setting. I helped the cooper check the barrels. Then, finally, night started to fall and the decks emptied out slowly.

It took me a while to realise that that was a bad thing: anyone who walked into our cabin would see my Siren. They'd chase her out, hurt her. In a panic, I thundered down the steps and slammed open the door, but she wasn't there. A couple of my crewmates looked at me, surprise or annoyance shaping their features, but no one said a word about a creature on board.

Where had she gone?

With an uneasy feeling in my stomach, I waited on my bedroll until the ship fell quiet. Then, feeling my way through the dark, I tiptoed back up the steps and to the quarterdeck.

I shouldn't have worried. There she was, standing by the main mast, her hand steady on the wood.

The night was quiet, the bright full moon our only witness. I could hear someone, somewhere on the deck, playing the lute. It was a joyful melody, something that didn't quite settle in my chest but hovered over it, a happiness that was just out of reach.

But then she saw me, and she smiled, and my chest filled with uncontainable joy.

"I'll miss this ship," she said, her fingers trailing a pattern down the wooden beam. "It has been very welcoming."

My joy dimmed. She was leaving. In a few minutes she'd be gone, and I'd never see her again.

Which is a good thing, I told myself. *She's a Siren. She belongs in the water. She's a danger to the rest of the crew. You're saving all of them by doing this. You're saving her.*

"It has been... an honour," I managed to say.

She chuckled, the sound mixing with the lute's melody. "How polite. That's a wholly different side of you than the one I saw this afternoon."

She pushed away from the mast and walked up to me. Her hand caressed my cheek, and it was as if a final puzzle piece slid into place — now, at last, I was complete.

"I'll go," she said then, her voice low. "But you could come with me?"

41

I stared at her. Half of my mind was caught up on how easy it would be to draw her closer, throw my arms around her neck, and lock my fingers. The other half had a hard time trying to make sense of her words. "Excuse me?"

A roll of the shoulder, a smile appearing on her scaled face. "Wouldn't you like that, Salina? The water is quite nice. It'll feel very warm once you get used to it, I promise."

I let out a nervous laugh as she trailed a finger down the side of my face.

"What are you afraid of?"

"I'm not afraid of anything." I leaned into her touch, but she moved away, dropping her hand.

"I have to go. The water is calling me. You were right. It is my home."

"I did try to tell you." Those strings between us tightened again, and I listened to them, followed her as she moved across the deck and to the chains. The entire time, I felt like I was walking among the clouds instead of on the rough wooden planks of *The Belle-Fleur*.

This afternoon, in between chores, I'd tied a rope ladder to the swing guns, and it was still there, hanging over the edge. I doubted my Siren needed a ladder to leave, but I wanted to take care of her.

She looked at me through her lashes. Drops of water were stuck in them, catching the moonlight and turning it into rainbows. "Will you miss me?"

"I'll miss you," I breathed.

"Good." She flowed past me, took hold of the ladder. She was really going to do it. She was really going to leave. And I'd be here, chasing Elio, chasing a mother who no longer cared about us — for what?

For Elio. For your brother.

The Siren swung one leg over the ship's edge, then the other. I stared at her from the top of the rope ladder as she went down, but she didn't look up at me once. I felt my heart drop over the railing with her, falling out of reach.

"Wait," my mouth said, and my hands were on the ropes, and my legs followed, and I clambered over and down, all the while looking at her.

And she still didn't return my gaze.

Without pause, she lowered herself into the water. Her legs morphed together, changing into a fishtail of dark green and deep blue. The scales reminded me of a spider's web, a complicated network of lines that felt perfectly whole yet wholly unpredictable. I remembered the feeling of her legs underneath my fingertips — and wanted more.

"Come," she said.

Perhaps, if I went with her, my own legs would change like that. Perhaps I'd be able to move through the water with the kind of freedom I'd always sought on a ship but never found.

I stepped off the ladder, dipped my toe in the ocean. I couldn't remember when I'd taken my shoes off, but it didn't really matter. I'd find them again. At some point. Later.

My foot disappeared beneath the surface, followed by my ankle, my shin, my knee. The muscles in my arms ached as I held on to the ladder's bars, my fingers hooked around the metal as if they were nervous, refusing my service.

Determined, I let one hand go. Told the nerves to go away. What was there to be nervous about, after all?

My eyes searched for her in the waves and found her right by the ladder, waiting for me. Finally, she was looking at me. She drifted in the water like a goddess, brighter than the moon.

43

Her glow filled me up, giving me the final push of confidence I needed.

I let go of the ladder and slid into the water completely. She was right. It did feel warm on my skin. Gentle — not at all as rough as the waves made it out to be. And then there was the saltiness, delicious on my tongue.

I leaned back, allowing my hair to get wet. For a moment, I stayed there, my eyes closed and my ears under the surface so I heard nothing but the thumping of my own heart.

When I lifted my head again, she was almost nose to nose with me. While my feet were constantly moving below me, always working to keep me up, she floated with ease. Her tail brushed past my ankles, and a shudder ran through me.

"Isn't it beautiful?" she said as I wrapped my arms around her neck. "Aren't you glad you joined me?"

Another shudder — and I realised I was shivering. Perhaps the water hadn't been so warm after all. So I pulled her closer. As long as I stayed with her, I'd be able to stay warm. I'd be safe. Because she was safety. She was perfection. She was...

She stared at me. I longed to touch her. To taste the salt on her lips, her skin. So I closed the gap between us and—

My arm hurt as something sharp dug into it. Deep.

As if in slow motion, I looked down, and saw that her hand — the hand that had held me so gently hours ago — had morphed into something different altogether. Something with talons that were buried into the flesh of my arm.

"What are you—"

She smiled, and her teeth were no longer human, either. They were thin and sharp, like a snake's.

As if waking from a dream, I no longer felt safe, or warm, or restful, or whole. I felt like prey, and I was already weakened.

44

"Aren't you glad you joined me?" she repeated, her breath foul.

I opened my mouth, gathering my breath to scream, but she dragged me down. The ocean closed above my head, the shimmering of the moon becoming smaller and smaller as I was pulled further away from the world I knew.

Her strong tail moved beside me with confident strokes while she held onto me like I was a rag doll.

There was an ache in my forehead, a strange dryness in my throat that begged me to open my mouth. I needed to go up. I needed to go up and get air and breathe and breathe and breathe but—

I thrashed, trying to get out of her grip. She sent a short, almost annoyed, glance over her shoulder, and I almost swallowed a mouthful of seawater. Her entire face had changed. She was no longer beautiful, no longer a human goddess. Instead, the face staring at me had slits for a nose, a lipless mouth, and monstrous eyes.

Let me go, I tried to say, but my words came out as mere bubbles, rising up and disappearing to the unreachable surface far above.

More thrashing. Pulling against her grip. Digging my nails in between her scales. But she kept going, and I was stuck. My brain got dizzy and I needed to *breathe* but I couldn't, and the world around me got so dark and this had to be it. These had to be my final moments.

Then she slowed her pace.

"I did tell you I like completing my collections," she said.

I didn't understand. Not at first. I was too preoccupied with the blood oozing from my wounds, merging with the water and turning it pink. But then I did, and felt my hopes sink faster than the rest of me.

With the Siren's talons still in a death's grip on my wrist, I saw him at the bottom of the sea, barely visible in the dark. Open eyes, brown like mine. Hair that used to be curly, now drifting lazily in the current. Chest torn open, a giant fish hook keeping him in place, body tangled up in seaweed.

There, at the bottom of the ocean, drifted the bloated body of my brother, the worn piece of a tartan dress clutched in his hand.

Another Chance

K. D. Bowers

A snake of a man gave me an evil wink from a nearby table. Dressed in a long-buttoned coat, and matching cream-colored-striped pants, he had dark wavy hair and a pointed goatee, and milky white eyes. He snapped his fingers, and a deck of cards appeared on the table in front of him, his milky gaze focused only on me. The other employees' eyes slipped from him, and I asked them if they witnessed this strange figure. They had blank expressions on their faces. So, I trusted my gut instinct and assumed I was the only one who could see him; he was invisible to everyone else in the lounge. I passed a few drunks by the jukebox singing Christmas songs and clinking their glasses and made my way to the man's table. The reek of spilled beer filled the air. I nervously placed a menu on the table. Closer up, I could see they were tarot cards.

"Hi... what can I get for you?" I asked.

He glanced down at my nametag. His voice was raspy and snakelike.

"Hello, Emma, it's good to meet you. My name is Ivan. Would you care to play a card game? A game that will *change* your life."

My stomach contracted into a tight ball. I had never seen him before. I'd been working at the Hideaway Tavern for over a year and knew all the locals. They were college freshmen that attended the university nearby. The males wore Oxford shirts, and the females dressed in turtlenecks. The tavern was on the main street of Brooklyn and brought in good business. The holidays were approaching, and a few unfamiliar faces stopped by occasionally.

I remained calm. "Am I the only one who can see you?" I asked.

"That's correct. Those who *can* see me are the ones suffering." His hairy hand looked more like a monkey's paw than that of a human. Ivan shuffled the deck once, drew five cards, and placed them face down on the table. "Point to a card, but don't pick it up."

I took a closer look at the cards. The artwork was in the Gothic style: red font on a black background, featuring mythological and occult symbolism. Ivan's game caught my interest. I wanted to play to see what happened next, and so, I went along with it.

"How does this game work?"

"It's simple. Choose a card. Your life will change forever. Destiny awaits."

Destiny? I choose from the far left. The card depicted the paw of a monkey — not unlike the hideous man's hand — turning black in a fire.

He picked the chosen card. "What loved one do you wish to bring back from the dead? You have three days to think about your answer."

Someone then tapped me on the shoulder. My boss.

"What the hell are you doing?" He asked, frowning.

48

The table was empty.

"I— I was talking to a man a few seconds ago." I motioned toward the seat.

He placed a hand on his hip. "Get back to work. Customers are waiting."

Thirty minutes later, my shift was over, and I drove back to my cramped studio apartment. My room was on the first floor of a two-story office building, the cheapest place I could afford. My front window faced a back alley, home to an assortment of rats and raccoons. I was met with my dishes from the last two days, still piled up in the sink. But every ounce of energy was gone. The dishes could wait another day. I stepped into my tiny bathroom. The one working bulb cast a dim light on the mold growing from wall to ceiling. Toothpaste was in the sink, and the shower looked grimy. I considered cleaning it, have considered it for weeks. Not tonight.

Back in the living room, boxes were stacked to the ceiling and bags of clothes were scattered by the front door. Maybe tomorrow I would take care of business. I slumped on the couch to watch TV, munching on some Chex Mix, my feet on the coffee table beside an empty container of ice cream and two crushed Budweiser cans. My prescribed medication lay on the dirty floor next to the couch. I left the Prozac there where it belonged. I didn't feel like taking any pills. Not tonight.

***

All the channels played traditional Christmas movies. I wanted to puke. I was sick of the holiday season and wanted it to be banished to hell for *an eternity*.

I couldn't stop thinking about what had happened earlier, about Ivan and the card game. I questioned my sanity. The holidays always leave me feeling exasperated.

* * *

It was the week before Christmas, a few winters ago when I was still in high school. The phone rang in the middle of the night. My parents answered, and I stood in the doorway, overhearing the police report the unfortunate news that would change my life. Tawnya, my older sister, had been killed in a car accident. She had hit a concrete barrier, drunk. The car was totaled. Her body was unrecognizable.

I couldn't believe my sister was gone, just like that. I wished I could have said a last goodbye. At her funeral, I realized that it should have been me that died in the crash.

Tawnya was the head cheerleader, prom queen, and President of the National Honor Society. The town loved her for the volunteer work she did in her spare time. She painted over old church fences; donated old and new clothes to the homeless shelter; planted trees in the neighborhood park; organized family dinners at the event center to raise money for charity; and volunteered as a leader at summer camp for the mentally disabled.

She loved to dance. She danced at school plays and competed in tournaments. Every weekend, they dropped her off at the dance club. My parents loved her more. She was always number one. As she danced effortlessly, twirling on her toes, my envy only grew worse. I wanted to break her legs so she would never dance again.

***

Instead, I got even in other ways. When she was nine years old, I stole her favorite Barbie doll. It looked like her: curly hair and dance leotards. I buried the doll in the back yard so she would never find it. I broke her reading glasses in middle school. I didn't take the blame. I lied to my parents. I had poisoned her pet goldfish and was never caught. I never forgave myself for that one. I was a lousy sister. And to top it off, the night she died, I had left the party early, even though I knew my sister had been drinking.

That year, I never put a present under the Christmas tree. I only thought of myself. Christmas that year was missing the holiday spirit. My parents wept around the tree and all the gifts were finally for me.

I shut off the misery on the TV and fell asleep.

* * *

At ten the next morning, I clocked in for my shift. I counted the money from the register, organized the pint glasses, and wiped down the bar counter. I was checking in the back-storage area for limes as Sandra came out of the freezer. In her small hands was a box of frozen patties.

Sandra had been a cook at the Hideaway Tavern since the eighties. Her father was an immigrant from Mexico and had moved to the United States in the 1950s. She was the hardest working employee in the joint. I had a better relationship with Sandra than my other coworkers. Last month, I'd had a mental breakdown after my shift. She listened. I told her how I ran away from home at age eighteen and didn't complete my senior year of high school. I felt like a burnout, didn't know what to do with my life.

"You are young. Have hope. Don't let your past interfere with your future."

Something about her eyes made me ask if she had ever encountered a man named Ivan. She tensed up, the box dropped from her hands, and she shook her head. She formed a closed-lipped smile.

"No. Don't talk to him. He's bad news. End of story."

51

I had struck a nerve.

"What? Y— you can see him too?" My voice shook. "Tell me about him."

"I'm telling you for your own good." Anger crept into her voice. "Find work someplace else. Leave while you still have a chance." Sandra grabbed the box from the floor and returned to the kitchen.

After my shift, I drove to the lake, Sandra's favorite spot. She was sitting on a bench, throwing seeds to the geese that drifted in the water nearby. The bright sun reflected off the water. I sat down beside her, zipping up my jacket and putting on my gloves to keep warm.

"What's the deal with Ivan?" I asked.

"Others have played his game," she spoke. "Past employees that came and went. Three years ago, a young man named Carson who used to bartend played the game. He had the choice of his desire — a million dollars. He wasn't so lucky, though. In exchange, he witnessed our old manager suffer a heart attack in the middle of his shift. He was dead by the time the ambulance arrived. The tavern was shut down for a month."

I waited. There was more.

"And then there was a girl who was... less fortunate." Sandra threw the last bit of seeds into the lake. "She wanted to get rid of her bad looks, be pretty. Ivan turned her into the most beautiful woman, but she paid the price. The next day, she turned to dust.

"I've made the mistake of playing his card game, too." The tone of her voice turned melancholy. "The card I got brought a loved one back from the dead. I brought my father home, but he wasn't the same man. He is an empty shell, no personality, like the color has been drained from his soul. He can't hold a spoon. He mumbles when he talks. I keep him locked in a room while I'm away. He stares at the wall all day long. In exchange, Ivan took away my best friend; I never saw her again.

"I'm sorry," I sympathized.

I looked away. Ob-La-Di, Ob-La-Da was carved into a tree by the lake. Life goes on. I should leave things be. The past was behind me.

I trusted Sandra. I had no desire to be turned to ash.

* * *

The next few days, the tavern was *packed*. I was exhausted and I wanted to go home. The Christmas music playing from the jukebox drained every inch of my being, the holiday earworms played in my head constantly, even after work.

I picked up my usual comfort remedies from the grocery store: a bag of Chex Mix and a can of Budweiser. On my drive back home, I saw a father and daughter strolling along the lake. The father was pointing to the lighthouse, but the daughter was too busy playing on her phone. I tightened my grip on the steering wheel and watched them disappear from my rearview mirror.

Dumb girl. One day your father is not going to be there. You probably won't know what you have until he's gone. No, your phone won't love you like your father does, you *naïve twat*.

* * *

I jumped in the shower to feel clean. I kept my eyes closed, so that I didn't have to see the mold on the walls. My thoughts ran wild like an untamed animal. I visualized Tawnya pulling back the shower curtain and grabbing me by the neck. She turned the hot water knob all the way with her other hand, and scalding water flowed over me, unbearably hot, and I felt my skin melting.

"Tell me you're sorry, Emma. I want to hear you say it! Tell me that you've done nothing but hurt me."

"I'm sorry!" I gasped for air. "I— I take it all back, T-Tawnya."

She turned off the hot water and I fell over on my side, my entire body covered in fresh blisters. Tawnya stood over me. *Please stop it. Leave me alone, thoughts.*

I tried to focus my attention on the present moment by breathing in slowly through my nose and slowly exhaling through my mouth. After a couple of minutes, the vision ceased.

* * *

The next day, I was smoking a cigarette behind the restaurant, when Ivan appeared from the shadows. Startled, I jumped.

"Did you think about your answer, dear?" He folded his hands and listened closely.

I had decided to trust Sandra's word, to not play Ivan's game. The stories she'd told me about the other employees was enough for me to say no. They'd each paid a terrible price, and it wasn't worth it.

"I've had a change of heart. Not interested. Have a good day." I turned to walk towards the entrance. He snapped his fingers; I was unable to move.

"What's the big idea? Let me go!"

"Did you think you could quit that easily?" He snickered. "If you don't play my game, I will have your parents killed. It's your choice, Emma. Play my game, and I won't harm them." He snapped his fingers, and I was free again.

There was nothing I could do. I wanted to run, but knew I was screwed. I didn't want my parents involved.

54

"Who do you want to bring back from the dead?" He hissed.

"I— I decided I want my sister back."

He rubbed his chin. "Why do you want to bring back your sister?"

"I did her wrong and want to make things right. I have learned from my mistakes. I was an idiot."

He nodded. "Very well. I will bring back your sister.Hold out your palms and close your eyes. Do not open them."

I did what he told me. I extended my hands outward and shut my eyes.

"Good. Now, say her name and think about your sister. What does she look like? What is she wearing? What is she doing?"

I said her name and dug deep. I imagined my sister's curly ginger hair and freckled face smiling at me. She was in an auditorium dancing in front of thousands of people; every seat was filled. The spotlight shone on her body, as she moved naturally to the upbeat tempo. The song then played faster; the melody got darker. A glass chandelier, which hung from the marble ceiling, swung. I couldn't stop my imagination; it took over.

No, *not* now. This is *not* the time. Go *away*, I thought. Go *away*.

Halfway through her set, Tawnya tripped and landed on her back. She grimaced in pain, holding her leg. The audience gasped as the chandelier dropped from the ceiling, landing on Tawnya. The glass splintered, spraying into the audience, as the spotlight dimmed and the curtains closed. My cursed imagination came to a halt. I opened my eyes, feeling like I'd just woken up from a bad dream.

"Done. Your sister, Tawnya will be back tomorrow. She will be waiting here for you." Ivan grinned. "Thank you for playing,

Emma."

"But why me?" I said, out of breath.

He laughed. "I wait for everyone to be at their breaking point to play. It was just your turn to play my game." He vanished into thin air.

* * *

I woke up from terrible, vivid dreams on Christmas Eve, feeling nervous. Out my front window, the town was covered in a blanket of snow. I did not know what to expect today. Since Ivan had forced me to play his game, I expected the worst to happen. If she did come back, would Tawnya be the same girl I used to know? Or would she end up like Sandra's father? I sighed. Maybe she wouldn't come after all, and I was worrying for nothing. I kept dwelling on the blackness. I thought about making breakfast, but I felt like I would throw it up. Instead, I got dressed for work and headed out. On the drive, my hands shook on the steering wheel the entire time and I couldn't stop grinding my teeth. Negative thoughts battered me, full force.

You're so stupid! You have made the worst decision of your life. Your sister is going to be a zombie. You're going to regret this for the rest of your life. Stop! I needed to silence those thoughts. Slowly, I counted to one hundred and felt at ease. Everything was going to be ok.

By the time I pulled into the parking lot, several police cruisers surrounded the Hideaway Tavern. I hurried out of my car and was abruptly stopped by an officer inside the front lobby, but what I could see made me want to scream. The Christmas tree had been knocked over, as well as several of the tables. The floor was scattered with bodies: my coworkers, my boss. Their throats had been slit. And then I saw Sandra. She

56

lay next to the jukebox. Her face was bruised and swollen, and she wasn't breathing. I tried to get to her, but the officer forced me out and walked me to my vehicle, no questions asked.

I drove to the lake and sat on the bench to collect my thoughts. I buried my face into my hands, trying to process what I had witnessed earlier. All of the memories I had with Sandra flashed by in a moment. She was gone, but I didn't want to believe it. The more I dwelled on the murders, the sicker and more guilty I felt. It should have been me. I never wanted to go near the tavern ever again.

I was sure that Ivan had something to do with the murders. He was behind this tragedy; maybe this was the price he exacted for our deal, or maybe he was just a madman and a murderer. I called the police station, but they wouldn't listen to me. Investigators were still looking into the case. When I finally raised my head, I looked up and saw a flock of birds flying across the lake. I wished I could fly away.

I got back into my car and started to drive back to my apartment, when, the next block over, I saw a tall girl with ginger hair walking down the street alone. It was my sister. I pulled over, and she got into the passenger seat. Tawnya wrapped her arms around me and squeezed. She looked exactly how I remembered her.

We talked for hours that night. I mentioned what had been bothering me all those years, and she forgave me. The mental wall inside me shattered. I was finally free from the guilt. It was comforting to know she was back in my life.

We hugged goodnight, and I climbed into bed. I turned on my side, to finally get a good, peaceful night's sleep. That was when I noticed the bloody knife under my pillow.

Little Dirt Boy

Erik McHatton

A week after the funeral, Agnes found one of his teeth. Her hand, stretched and sightlessly padding about the bottom of a stubborn drawer, fumbled across it while searching for a favored pair of sewing scissors. Her chest and stomach tightened as she pulled the small thing out and fresh tears came quick and hot as it rolled around her palm. It was the one he'd lost while trying to jump from the rope swing his father, James, had made for him. *This was in his head once,* she thought dizzily while clutching it against her chest and falling heavily to the floor. The rest of the afternoon was spent sobbing, the sewing, abandoned.

A week later, she got an idea. It hit her as she lay in bed, battling for another night the insomniatic curse that had plagued her since his death. Inspired, she hurriedly found and took down the old Dutch packer trunk left to her by her mother. She tore through the pile of mouldered dresses and shoes before finally finding the family almanac she'd tucked away at the bottom.

Adding to the book had been her sweet mother's favorite pastime, and in her waning years had become almost an obsession. Agnes had added nothing to the record since receiving it, a fact that bothered her only a little. She had no patience for silly things, and even less for most people, so naturally nothing seemed sillier to her than keeping the useless history of no-count people living in a no-count place. Upon inheriting it, however, Agnes found she couldn't bear to throw it out. After finding the page she went excitedly searching for, she was certainly glad she hadn't.

What she looked for was an example of what her mother had referred to as "hilltop devilry," one of the arcane practices of the ancient hill people from which her family descended. The ragtag tome was filled with primitive, hand-me-down recipes, spells and cures, along with esoteric rituals that were only sensible to the superstitious and the gullible, the weak and the desperate. While Agnes considered herself neither superstitious nor gullible, the death of her son had left her weakened, driven to desperation by despair. Her grief threatened every moment to consume her as it continuously chewed at her mind. This was why she sought the hilltop magic that day, why she attempted to conjure a little dirt boy.

It was so very simple. She had but to wrap the tooth in a scrap of his clothing — after first covering it in a slew of herbs and oils — and then place the bundle inside a large ball of mud. Next, a burial in the back garden, followed by precise chanting for well over an hour. The book's instructions called for only a quarter of that time, but Agnes needed to be sure. If there was even the slightest chance a part of her dear boy's spirit could be returned to her, she vowed not to ruin it. Finishing the recital, she kneeled an hour longer before the newly wrought grave, and prayed to gods she claimed not to believe in with an intense, belying fervor.

That night, when she finally won her sleep, she dreamed of the awful incident that had stolen her child away.

They had walked deep into the expanse of woods behind the old barn, set once again on his never ending quest for woodland oddments to marvel over. Agnes marvelled at his amazement each time he uncovered some new curiosity hidden amongst the dead leaves and branches. Be it a hollowed turtle shell, sun-bleached and beaming, or a tragic nest of broken eggs, he never failed to be astonished by his discoveries. Precocious and full of wonderment, he led her slowly on little fat legs and she followed, soaking up as much of him as she could.

He had been disappointed to reach the ridge at the end of the old trail. He never liked the conclusion of their explorations, but this time was especially frustrating as he had found nothing new to add to his collection. He sputtered about the clearing, red-faced, and complained to the heavens with two tiny, balled fists. She stifled a laugh as he moved around in furious circles, and tried to calm him, but he was tired and could not have his tiny tantrum tamped down. Then he saw the bird.

Dried and maggoty, the body of a blackbird crowned a bed of moss at the base of a tree that hung precariously at the edge of the ridge. He picked it up before she could stop him and began to squish it between his hands, laughing. He'd never held a dead thing before, and didn't understand the difference between life and nonlife. She was horrified at the slithering pupae squirming between his fingers, at the dead bird's eye falling over his knuckles. She cried out, and rushed toward him, knocking the putrid thing from his grasp. Startled, he stumbled. Stumbling, he fell over the lip of the ridge, and the only thing she managed to catch was one of his little red shoes as he tumbled, bounced and screamed through the dense, disfiguring branches to the unforgiving ground below.

***

She couldn't recall recovering his body or her frenzied flight into the village. That part is only ragged breaths, burning pain and a cloud of overwhelming fear. Of her search in vain for help, only snippets remained, the swirling dreamfog carrying her swiftly from impression to impression with no real feeling of anything other than unrelenting guilt and misery. She always ended up in the same place, however, dumped unceremoniously into a graveside seat in the family cemetery, staring at its newest hole intent on swallowing another of her loved ones. They'd dug it out between James' grave and her mother's, in the plot originally meant for her. *I killed him and gave him my grave*, she thought, pulling dully at her hair.

In the dream, as in reality, she was held tightly as she strained to reach the lowering coffin — held as she wailed, as she bargained, as she fainted. This is where the dream usually ended, with Agnes shooting up in her bed, lathered and panting. Not this night. On this night, she spurned the well-meaning graspings of her friends and neighbors and fell headlong into the hole after her child. She plummeted for what seemed like eternity before crashing down atop his earth covered casket. Recovering, she threw fistfuls of dirt over her shoulder, slinging it in all directions, before finally exposing the lid and prying it open with raw fingers.

He was there, sticky with sap and blood, his dead eyes looking up at her accusingly, akimbo arms splayed like a ghoulish marionette. Now, she remembered. He appeared just as he had when she'd found him at the bottom of the ravine and just as then she gathered him up and cradled him, weeping and apologizing profusely. Placing him on one shoulder, she

61

attempted to climb out of the pit, crying to those above for help. Answering these cries came a rain of detritus as those above began to fill in the hole, and she slowly suffocated as she held her dead son and cried.

Her heart hammering, she awoke, mistaking the pounding in her ears for a banging at the front door. She rushed to open it and there, on the doorstep, sitting exactly as he had, legs tucked beneath it, was a little dirt boy.

She squatted to survey it. Trepidatious, she gently prodded, testing its solidity, entertaining thoughts of encroaching insanity. Her finger came back mud-streaked and damp, much to her surprise. Doubts allayed, she rocked back on her bottom and folded her own legs beneath her in order to consider the thing properly.

Much more than superficially it resembled her son. This resemblance shone like the sun and she found the need to look away several times to avoid a rising sorrow. Its muddy head was round like his, its face rightly lumpy in the nose places, the eye places, the lip places, the ears. Vegetative sprouting at the top suggested his ever-mussy hair, and its reedy appendages were draped inquisitively across its branchy lap in his manner of storytime readiness. Its trunk was rounded, insinuating an overly indulged appetite for sweets, and sticking straight out of its lump-mouth was an oily tooth, no doubt the one from which the golemic creature had spawned.

Satisfied, she scooped it up, ignoring her mud stained clothes, and joyfully brought it inside.

The next several days flew by in a delirious haze. Agnes felt nearly whole again in the company of the little dirt boy, and in no time at all she settled into a routine that almost perfectly mirrored the one she had enjoyed with her son before his death. Aside from a few snags relating to its lack of appetite and animation, and the extra cleaning now required due to its pervasive filthiness, her life soon returned to an unsteady tranquility. If not for the tremulous feeling of wrongness just outside the borders of her sanity, she could have sworn that things were back to normal for her, and the part of her son with which she now lived.

When she told it stories before they retired to bed each night, she imagined a slight smile crossed its irregular features. On the occasions that she took it walking in the woods, carrying it in a makeshift sling across her back, she was quite sure of the small yips and trills that it made when she pointed out wondrous things tangled in the flora. When preparing its favorite foods for their dinners (meals only she ate), she could just hear a growling coming from deep within its bulbous belly. In response to the announcement that there would be no more baths to worry about, she distinctly heard a small whooping from behind her while she caught up on the extra laundry at the creek. It spoke to her in its own way, and she was keenly receptive to it as only a mother could be.

Unsure of how much of her son's memory the thing retained, she filled its days with tales of their recently lost family so as not to be the only one who remembered them.

On one afternoon, they visited the rope swing and laughed as she told of her hysteria at the profuse bleeding that followed its accident there. She reminded it of its father's kind words and manner as he managed the situation with his soft, calming hand. She then wistfully recounted several other delightful accounts of James' good humor, of his kind heart, and of his generous wealth of spirit. After being reminded herself of how dear their James had been, she decided to walk it up the road to the abandoned wheat mill to show it where its father was working when he met his end not two years prior, and just like the day after James' funeral, she threw rocks at the sagging vanes, whooping and hollering with the dirt boy all the while.

She told it of her mother, and how wonderful it had been to have her live with them following James' accident. She made it berry tarts and baked apples, her mother's specialties, and even read to it from the family almanac in deference to her memory. She dressed it in clothes her mother had made for it and sat with it in her mother's rocker while singing songs her mother loved, and which she claimed were as old as the hills themselves. She told it much about the good year they enjoyed together before the wretched illness, before the devouring of her mother's body and mind. She didn't speak to it of those last few months, of course, no reason to remind it of that, but she could not help remembering herself the face of the gaunt, shrieking creature her mother became. It was a face she and she alone would forever keep, locked away deep within.

She didn't dwell too much on her sorrows, preferring laughter and revelry to morose recollection. In those days she came to love the dirt boy almost as much as her living son, and its company balmed the fierce aching that had previously threatened to overtake and drive her into the ground as well.

***

She enjoyed almost a month of this new life before the pastor called upon them.

His coming was heralded, as ever, by the warbling whistle he was so fond of employing when making his rounds about the village and surrounding farms. She knew that a man of the cloth would never approve of hilltop devilry, and that the busybodies in the village just loved to gossip about such things, so as he breached her front gate and made his way down the walk, Agnes stowed the little dirt boy inside the packer trunk, right atop her mother's old things. She had just managed to cover with a sheet the tainted kitchen chair wherein the dirt boy usually sat, when the pastor's friendly knocking came fluttering at the door.

"Agnes dear, it's Pastor Willoughby callin'. I came to see how you are. No one in the village has heard from you since the funeral and Ethel and the girls in the choir are simply beside themselves with worry. Oh, do please let me in, if only to allow me to rest a while before I have to head back into town. It's powerful hot out here you know, beneath the mighty sun of God," he caroled in a singsong voice, chuckling at his clerical pun.

She considered not answering. She was never one of his congregants, but he had presided over her many funerals for free, and had been comforting to Agnes when she had needed it the most. Reluctantly, she opened the door and afforded the pastor a broad smile.

"Pastor, how good of you to stop by. Come in, please, and sit with me in the kitchen. I'll put on some tea."

"Why, thank you my dear, it would be a pleasure," huffed Willoughby as he squeezed his bulk through the cabin's small door and waddled after Agnes into the kitchen. As she busied herself with the tea, he plopped down into the unsheeted seat at the table and began dabbing at his brow with an embroidered handkerchief produced from his breast pocket. By the time the kettle crowed, he had regained much of his composure and his breathing had become notably less labored.

Accepting a steaming cup from her, Willoughby blew across its top before taking a careful sip. Scrunching his nose, he gave a loud "Woo!" into the air as Agnes took the sheeted seat across from him for herself. The moistness beneath seeped through and she hoped the pastor couldn't hear the soft squishing sound being made by her anxious shifting.

"My dear you always did make a fantastic cup of tea. Those old women in the village just don't know anythin' about the careful removal of bitterants," he said through a doughy smile filled with large, gleaming teeth, "but you darlin', you know just how to brew it."

He tipped the cup in her direction before taking another sip and giving another dramatic "woo." Grunting, he languidly stretched his legs before him and sighed. Sniffing at the air, he settled his gaze on Agnes as if waiting for a reply to a question he hadn't asked. Several moments went by, and his small eyes never wavered. Agnes squirmed within that uncomfortable silence that he seemed so very comfortable inside of.

"I've been doing quite well, you know. Quite well. I understand why those of you in the village might worry, what with James, and mother... and with my boy, but I'm managing quite well, quite well indeed. You needn't worry about me," she finally blurted, as she took a wobbling drink from her cup.

"Darlin', I had little doubt that would be the case, but you know how those girls get when they circle up for gossip. You know how annoying they can be once there's a buzzin' in their bonnets. So I told them I'd come by and see you, to put their minds at ease, and also to save you from having to host the lot of them before the week was out. They don't think a woman can get by without a man to see to things, it's just how they are. No matter that I told them what a tough little girl you were, or about the tough woman you've become, they wouldn't have it unless I agreed to check," said Willoughby, finishing off his tea and putting away his handkerchief.

"Well, you tell 'em they have nothin' to worry about," said Agnes, subconsciously mimicking the pastor's drawl. "Tell 'em I'm doin' juuuuuuust fine."

Sniggering, Willoughby leaned forward and took Agnes' tight fists in a damp grip. He shook them up and down exuberantly.

"I will. I'll tell 'em I seen you with my own eyes and that your house was spotless as could be. I'll tell 'em that the front lawn was perfectly manicured, and that you made me some tea better than any pot they ever brewed. That'll stick right in their craws, I bet!" He chortled before pausing, his face becoming serious as he afforded her with another prolonged look. Without hesitating this time, Agnes cut right through it.

"What?" she said, somewhat harsher than she meant.

"Would you want to walk up to your old family cemetery with me right quick? I'd like to pay my respects to them of yours that's up there, to your momma and James… and to your boy too, if you'd like," he said solemnly.

Agnes took a moment, pretending to consider the offer she had no intention of taking. She didn't want anyone from the village anywhere near where her child had been buried, and after the nightmare she suffered before the coming of the little dirt boy, she didn't much care for the thought of going up there herself. Just thinking about it made her chest hurt.

"Thank you pastor, but I don't think I'd like that. I do appreciate the kind offer though, and the next time I'm able to get up there I'll be sure to bring them your respects."

"I understand," he said, standing slowly with a groan. Restoring the affable grin he'd worn into the house, Willoughby clapped her on the shoulder before making his way back to the front door. Agnes trailed behind so as not to show the soiled wetness at her back, seepage from the covering sheet. When reaching the front step he turned to her, his deep concern barely hidden.

"You take care of yourself, you hear, and if you need anythin' don't you be afraid to come and ask," he said, sniffing the air again before turning and heading down the cobblestone path. Without looking back he waved his hand theatrically over his head, saying finally, "You might want to check your attic dear, smells like something mighta' crawled in there and died."

As Agnes watched him disappear, whistling down the dirt road heading back into the village, she absentmindedly tugged at the grimy back of her sundress and had a sniff herself, only then smelling the smell she hadn't smelled at all before he'd come and smelled it for her; the musky scent of old rot.

The stench bedeviled her every moment after the pastor's visit. She and the dirt boy searched the house for days, top to bottom, side to side, and could find no source whatsoever. The attic and root cellar held a number of desiccated things: rats, insects, small birds and such, but this was common in country homes. None of those corpses appeared new enough, or large enough, to give off the wretched smell from which there was now no escape.

Eventually, nonplussed and frustrated, she settled on the idea of airing out the house and filling it with bouquets of fresh-picked wildflowers in order to combat the stink. Unfortunately, there was no place on her land more suited for picking perennials than the open fields of the back acre, the ones set right against the hill on which the family cemetery was located. Regardless of this fact, and almost in defiance of it, she planned a picnic there for her and her dirt boy, vowing to not so much as look up to that detestable hill while they took in what was sure to be a delightful outing.

As she left the reeking, unshuttered house the next morning, the limp boy slung carefully over her back, Agnes smiled into the dawnlight and swung her stuffed picnic basket with brisk exuberance. Some time later, they crested the southern slope that led to the field, and she stopped for a moment to consult with the dirt boy about just which spot they should spend their day upon. When satisfied with its answer, she made her way to it and spread out a checked blanket, emptying the basket before propping the dirt boy carefully against it.

She'd brought a smorgasbord of treats for them (her) to enjoy. A bottle of his favorite cider found secreted away in the root cellar was to be paired with a quarter wheel of cheese whose smell she was now slightly dubious of. Dried dates and currants and a loaf of day old bread rounded out the bounty along with the pièce de resistance, a marvelous summer sausage made earlier in the year for just such an occasion. While nodding at a job well done, she looked to the dirt boy for its approval of her offerings. Its head was crooked to the side, but the queer smile it sometimes seemed to give was evident on its knobby face. This pleased her, and she ate and talked and laughed with it for several hours under the bright, unclouded sky.

Later, while filling her empty basket with wildflowers, she caught herself glancing up the hill despite vigorous promises not to. With every surreptitious peek came nightmare flashes that stole her breath and left her weak. Glimpses of a midnight flight through the fields and away from the hill. Fleeting feelings of being overburdened with madness while covered in sweat and soil. She severely bent or outright broke several stems in her contracting hands as she tried to calm herself and focus. It had indeed been a bad idea to come here, and she decided to leave and make do with what flowers she'd managed to not destroy.

Hastily, she returned to the blanket where she'd left the dirt boy to nap and violently shooed away a blackbird she found picking at its head. Gathering it up along with their things, she gave a final involuntary look to the hill, to its spiked crown of broken fencing, and shivered before making her way down the winding trail back home.

Getting back, she found the smell in the cabin to be markedly subdued. Delighted, she set the dirt boy in his kitchen chair and began vasing and placing the flowers about the house at precise intervals before moving on to the reshuttering process. When reaching the window nearest the front door she spied the head busybody, Ethel Stone, ambling up the road toward her house carrying a covered pie. As she was no doubt intent on vacuous meddling, Agnes slammed the shutters, barred the door and dashed to the kitchen in order to block the final aperture. In her haste she tripped and crashed headlong into the dirt boy, bowling it over and spilling it onto the floor.

Crying out, she picked it up and apologized profusely, stroking its brittle vegetable hair and kissing it as she moved to close the kitchen shutters. There was Ethel, pie dropped and stupidly gawking across the yard, still behind the fence. Placing the dirt boy quickly out of sight, Agnes attempted a casual wave which Ethel returned with an aghast, over the shoulder gaze as she hurriedly turned and headed back in the direction of the village.

She was discovered.

Her insides knotted as she had an insane vision of a rowdy,

torch bearing mob descending on her cabin, intent on righteous witch burning. She imagined Pastor Willoughby's fat hands wrapped around his holy book, bellowing in pious fury while fixing her with a rage-filled glare. She knew it was a silly thought, and she hated herself for it, but something inside her knew that the way she'd been carrying on was wrong, knew she should be punished for the blasphemy her life had become. She'd been attributing this feeling to her mother's superstitious parenting, to the indoctrination she'd endured during childhood and never fully been rid of. But looking at the dirt boy now, slumped over on the counter, she couldn't deny a deep and soulful shame.

***

By the time she was lying next to the dirt boy that night, she was feeling much better. She'd spent the evening stoking fires of resentment for those in the village. After casting off her brief, ignominious sentiment, she wondered how it was that they dared to make her feel it in the first place. The nerve of them galled her.

"So what?" she said aloud, staring up at the ceiling. "So what if they know about you. It's my business what I do in my own home anyway. I'm not even part of the village, technically, a fact that they've never been too shy to remind me of. It shouldn't matter to them what goes on here. Bunch of busybodies is all they are, showing fake concern whenever there's trouble, never really helping. They just want something to talk about in that church of theirs every Sunday, something to make them feel superior, to distract them from their awful, no-count lives. I don't need them. I've never needed them, and I certainly haven't needed them these last few years.

"When your father died, and they brought his maimed body

to me, I sent them away and cleaned him up myself. I'd have made the box he went in too if they hadn't done it first. I'd have dragged him up to that damned cemetery and single-handedly put him in the ground just to be spared their pretending prayers and moronic condolences. Mother talked me out of it. She talked to me about 'community' and the 'brotherhood of man.' Pah! She trusted them too much, I told her so, and they proved me right.

"None of them, save the pastor and Doc Sutter, came to call when your grandmother got sick. They weren't here at the end as she raved and soiled herself endlessly. They didn't clean her, took no shifts so that I could sleep. No, they just sent messages and bland food, no doubt to placate their own guilt. But I managed well enough until there was nothing left of her to manage at all and then, of course, they came. They came with more platitudes and prayers, bearing a fresh pine box to feed that ravenous hill. It was all I could do to keep from spitting on them.

"I should never have run to them when you had your accident. Now they think I've invited them in. Now they think they have a right to be involved. Let them come, then, and I'll tell them all, even Pastor Willoughby, to leave me in peace and never bother us again."

She turned on her side and looked at the thing to affirm her rantings. The dirt boy gave only a dull, vacant stare.

"You never hold up your side of the conversation," she said, laughing softly to herself as she pulled it close and drifted off into troubled sleep.

***

The next day, of course, they came. A delegation comprised of several men from the village marched up the road, headed up by the pastor, Ethel Stone and old Doc Sutter. To a one, their faces were ugly with concern. She saw them long before they breached her gate and she prepared for their arrival accordingly. By the time they were on the front walk she had closed and latched all the windows and barred the front door. *Damn them and their false faces,* she thought as she sat down in the kitchen, clutching the little dirt boy so hard that it oozed.

There was a firm knocking at the door. No fluttering for Pastor Willoughby this day.

"Agnes dear," he said, trying and failing to keep his tone light, "please do let us in. Ethel swears she saw something terrible up here yesterday, something that can't possibly be true, and we just want to put her mind at ease. I know this is an awful imposition, but if you could let us inside we can have all this cleared up in a jiff."

"No, I don't think I will, Pastor. I… *appreciate* your concern, but I have no desire to ease Ethel's meddlesome mind and I don't feel I owe any of you any explanation for what I do in my own home. Now, if you please, I'd see you all off my porch and off my property. Go back to your village and pray for me if you wish, it's what you do best anyway," said Agnes, loud enough for them to hear.

The pastor's next words were more firm, less friendly.

"Now, dear, I'm afraid I'm going to have to insist. Doc Sutter is here with us and he's concerned as well, for your health, you understand. He just wants to check in and see how you are. Ethel's got him all a-tizzy with her imaginings."

"I seen what I seen," Ethel screeched, and Agnes was overcome with an urge to choke the life from her. Fire ran through her veins.

"GO AWAY," bellowed Agnes. "GET OFF MY LAND, YOU USELESS BUSYBODIES. WHAT HAPPENS HERE IS MY BUSINESS AND I'LL HAVE NO MORE OF YOUR GOD-DAMNED MEDDLING IN IT."

She heard the pastor exclaim "Oh dear," and then, after a brief moment of hurried whispering, there came a tremendous pounding against her door as the men outside sought to batter it down. Agnes began screaming obscenities and barely coherent curses, insisting they had no right, but they did not heed her. Within moments, the door splintered and the conclave came pouring into her home. They tromped determinedly through the house before finally streaming into the kitchen where they all stopped abruptly, gasping nearly in unison in horror at the sight of her. Ethel vomited, then fainted away.

"Fine, have a look if you want you bastards," she cried, holding the dirt boy before her, peeling it away from her defiled breast, "it's just a little dirt boy, a bit of hilltop devilry I conjured up to help me get by. I'm not hurting anyone, you see? So now that you've seen it, now that you've had your fill of gossip, pick that witch up off my floor and get out of my DAMNED HOUSE!"

Shocked beyond speech, they advanced and she recoiled from their encroaching, well-meaning grips, gnashing her teeth while attempting to shield the thing she now held behind her.

Then she was back within the nightmare, grasped and held firm while they pried what was left of her son from her arms. She screamed until hoarse as they carried her down the road toward the village, straining so hard she nearly broke her arms in the effort to free herself. Her mind unraveled as she watched two of the men leave her cabin, along with Pastor Willoughby, for they bore with them a carefully swaddled body. Consciousness was driven from her by the thought of where they were going with it, and what they meant to do.

They meant to travel the winding path and cross the wildflower field. They would climb to the top of that cursed and dream fogged hill where all her loved ones lay. They would seek the hole that in her maddening grief had been exhumed, that darkened pit wherein they would replace the last of her worldly joy. They would bury it again, and she would be damned by their best intentions.

Ghostly Visions

Matthew Anthony Allair

Rogelio Espinoza was a cautious man. He was not prone to accepting rumors or superstitions at face value, but when the stories came back to him about this rediscovered piece of art by Francisco Goya, believed to be part of his Peninsular War / Black Paintings, he was intrigued. He was piqued to follow the connection to a man from Madrid named Jesus De Leon who knew a man with direct knowledge of something, it was implied, extraordinary. Little was known about the painting, but Jesus implied there was a supernatural history about Goya's work from that period that left Rogelio intrigued enough to return an answer to the letter he had received from Mr. De Leon.

Rogelio was an art historian who had taken an interest in work that predated the surrealist movement. He often wondered if the imagination of the artists was a form of channeling and that some high power was speaking to them, and if so, that such channeling could be an affirmation of the spiritual world. Or perhaps a part of some collective unconscious as described by Jung. Rogelio often found that the muse was hard to define in the human psyche, was it sheer imagination or something more. To the ardent skeptic or atheist, the suggestion that otherworldly forces acted as muses was anathema to modern society. Rogelio found he had to suppress his more esoteric notions from academic peers, and some of his travels had to be more discreet and paid by himself outside of the benefits of his university professorship.

When Mr. De Leon had offered to provide lodging at a villa outside of Madrid, it was too great a temptation to decline. Because Goya had lived in Madrid in the late seventeenth century, and that alone could give Rogelio a wealth of insight into the painter's life and hopefully a glimpse of the times that Goya lived. Yet there were some things about Mr. De Leon's approach that were mysterious. Jesus only relied on emails and would not phone text. The only reason why Rogelio did not think he was a fraudster was due to their phone conversation and a few brief phone video chats. Plus Mr. De Leon's bona fides checked out: his background check, visual confirmation that he had a Facebook and Twitter account, and Jesus' record as an art collector.

Within a matter of weeks from their first correspondence they met in the town of Toledo before heading towards Madrid. A driver had been waiting for Rogelio when he departed his flight. Once his luggage had been collected the driver who only spoke the native tongue drove Rogelio to a small hotel that was modest. Jesus met him in the lobby with a broad smile.

"Señor," Jesus spoke pleasantly, "I hope your flights and travels were pleasant enough."

"Yes, indeed, Señor De Leon," Rogelio replied courteously, yet with some confusion as to why they were meeting there.

"The travel to the villa by car will take half a day," Jesus stated, Rogelio sensed that Jesus might anticipate his next question.

"We should enjoy the night and start fresh in the morning.

The drive should be good for both of us. I have much to tell you."

"Yes," Rogelio responded, "You implied there is a man we should meet, but I was unclear about the details."

"Yes, Señor," Jesus retorted effusively, "We can discuss this tomorrow. You must be tired after flying from Chicago. Is it true what they say about it, 'The Windy City?'"

"Yes, Señor," Rogelio acknowledged, "The wind can be a bear during the colder months."

Jesus gestured for him to follow him in a graceful manner to their adjacent rooms within the hotel's upper level.

The following morning, they ate a light breakfast and the porter loaded up Rogelio's luggage, and they headed off to the small villa. How far it was from Madrid, Jesus wouldn't say, but the silence was broken by their periods of conversation as they passed small towns and farmland.

"I brought lithographs of Goya's work from that period. Is this represented in what I have seen?" Rogelio inquired.

"Possibly not, Señor, it is believed to have been painted in 1801," Jesus replied. "I was told the title is 'Ghostly Vision', yet I am most eager for you to meet this older gentleman. His story is half of the story."

"This gentleman has knowledge of many things, Señor." Jesus responded, "His name is Lorenzo Moreno."

"So, Lorenzo's ancestors had a relationship with Goya then?" grilled Rogelio.

"In a manner of speaking, Señor," Jesus acknowledged with a smile.

Little else about the painting was discussed as they traveled. Rogelio sensed that Jesus, despite his friendly nature, was being guarded about this meeting and this man. He had doubts this wouldn't turn out to be some kind of fraudulent situation, a case of smoke and mirrors, which ends up being nothing more than a pleasant diversion. He wasn't holding out much hope that this could be some new and groundbreaking revelation about Goya's work from that period. The accounts were that the Peninsular war, when Napoleon lead the French army into Spain, had profoundly impacted Goya while he was living in Madrid. The psychological impact could be compared to the impact of World War I, a century later. It may have lead Goya down some strange paths. The tyranny of Napoleon had altered many assumptions and left many with broken promises, another despot who simply replaced other despots.

Rogelio learned a lot about Mr. De Leon while they drove. Jesus started as an aspiring painter when he was younger, but he only managed to get as far as a few community exhibits. He sold only a few paintings. He gradually evolved into an art curator who was drawn towards more exotic works. From there his reputation grew past Latin America and he had the means to travel the world looking for rare and unique work. By the time he had reached Rogelio about this work, he had negotiated multi-million dollar deals, and secured the rights to get works into high-profile museums.

While they traveled from town to town, community to community, a succession of small and older buildings, they would frequently pass churches and cemeteries littered with cypresses. They would often pass holm oaks, juniper, pine trees, thyme, and rosemary plants. In spite of the clutter of the towns, it did manage to feel bucolic. Rogelio felt a mixture of feelings, both awe and melancholy about being in this part of Old Europe. Like other regions of the planet, there was a struggle to embrace the old with the new, and the influence of the west was inescapable. The events of two hundred years earlier seemed so remote, Rogelio wondered if he could learn from the past when, in the hustle and bustle of the now, few could process what they saw, much less understand.

Conventional wisdom has assumed that Goya's work from 1819 to 1822 — these depictions of insanity, mental asylums witches, and fantastical creatures – were the culmination of disillusionment over religious and political corruption. So much so that by the 1820s Goya was living in near isolation. Yet Jesus' conversations implied something greater was at work. Rogelio wanted to believe in something greater, yet he had never seen any empirical evidence to support the existence of God, or something beyond the known universe. In this way, Rogelio could identify with Francisco Goya, a man who seemed adrift, perhaps had seen too much to believe that God had not abandoned all ages ago. Goya's demise and passing was both sad and mysterious. He was buried and his body was re-interred in Madrid, only to find that Goya's head went missing.

They stopped in the small town of Grinon for a rest and found a disturbing sight. An open coffin held a body with a missing head. One of the locals told them that the man had gone missing two weeks earlier. It could have been something related to the criminal underworld, but it was indeed surprising as the town had few issues with violent crime. Yet the parallel was disturbing for Rogelio, and he had to ponder if this was a harbinger of the upcoming days. Yet, since death was a normal occurrence in this world, it was likely just happenstance. After an espresso they loaded back into the car and continued.

"It won't be very much longer, Señor" Jesus assured Rogelio

to appease his restlessness. "The villa is in Colmenar Viejo; it is a nice little place and quiet."

It indeed didn't take long to reach Colmenar Viejo, and the villa was a very old, quaint single dwelling. The driver helped them with luggage as they passed a very old fountain. The ripple of the water was soothing. The outside walls were adorned with ivy, rosemary, bluebells and paula geraniums. Part of the villa had a courtyard, but once inside, one could find a large open set of windows and a balcony that overlooked the landscape at the other end of the small building. In the distance were a group of open steep hills. The villa was placed on a hill that overlooked the flea market that was known across the land.

Rogelio was shown into a small guest room.

"I will be staying nearby, Señor. You have this all to yourself." Jesus spoke brightly.

It was lovely and did represent some parts of old Europe that Rogelio didn't really see in the States. As much as Latin America represented its own ancient heritage, the age and historical weight of visiting Spain left one with a different feeling. Rogelio noticed that there was a painting on an easel that was covered up in this part of this house. He found himself drawn to it with sheer curiosity.

"Señor, I suggest you wait until Lorenzo arrives," Jesus advised as he approached him and stepped towards the shrouded painting. "He will help you to understand its importance."

Rogelio was puzzled over such wording as 'importance'. *How could this be any more significant than his other work with the Black paintings or his Peninsular War period work?*

Rogelio pulled out his book lithographs of Goya's paintings and thumbed through them. Jesus looked at him.

"Lorenzo should be here soon, Señor."

He hoped that these mysteries would be revealed soon. Not thirty minutes later, but after sundown, the old man, Lorenzo Moreno, knocked on the door, and Jesus allowed him in. The old man was very thin, and short. His hairline had wisps of hair left, and his clothing was baggy and loose. They exchanged pleasantries, but the old man spoke very little for half an hour. As Jesus seemed to be able to get him to warm up, this felt awkward to Rogelio, as no one had approached the covered painting as of yet. Then the old man gave Jesus a nod as he stood up and walked over to the easel and revealed the painting.

The painting had muted earth colors. In the center there was a large, dark figure, robed with long, thin hair, and horns. Its face was vague and non-distinct. It stood almost impassively, but it was unsettling to Rogelio. Another identical figure stood to its left in the frame. They both loomed over the unclear shapes of foreground figures. There seemed to be some solid complex to the lower right of the image, like some temple. *Was this a depiction of Purgatory?* Rogelio thought, *or Hell?*

"This painting had been missing since 1938. It has a power, doesn't it?"

Rogelio was puzzled: "Senor De Leon, this predates his Black Painting period or even the Colossus. This makes little sense."

"There is a reason, Lorenzo will explain."

Lorenzo spoke slowly as he began the tale. "Francisco had a friend named Pablo, an older mysterious man that few knew anything about. He would come and go. They met around 1800, and Pablo shared the truth of his gift, or curse, depending on how you see it."

"Which gift would this be?" Rogelio challenged.

"Pablo was tormented by visions of the spirit world, not only communicating with the dead, but spirits, ghosts, and visions of other worlds."

"Interesting, Goya is said to have been tormented by depression and mental illness."

"Pablo sensed that about Francisco, there was a bond. Some of the images of giants over a landscape, for example, or the Saturn painting. Some of the images depicted various angels of death. They were insights that Pablo offered Francisco, and he painted them."

Then the old man walked over to the painting.

"But in this painting, it is whispered, it depicts the angels of the apocalypse. It is said that once some mortal saw these angels with their own eyes, they would soon face their demise."

"Yet some of Goya's work was painted two decades later."

"Yes, Pablo must have worked out a bargain with the spirits, an agreement that gave him many more years."

"But this doesn't explain the gaps between various works."

"Ah, Señor Espinoza, but Pablo would travel from town to town, and wouldn't see Francisco for many years. He was a hermit, and for a good reason. It is said that Goya knew that Pablo believed his time was short when they first met, when he shared that vision with Goya. Some of these other worlds that Francisco painted may have been purgatory, or worlds beyond ours."

Jesus interjected. "It is said that Francisco was very disturbed by the Peninsula War. He lived in Madrid at the time, and it affected him deeply. Some even say that his deafness that came up after his illness in 1793 was an act of divine intervention."

Rogelio already knew this, but he was a little taken that Jesus was so ready and willing to accept Lorenzo's accounts.

"You see, Señor, Pablo was a great distant cousin of mine,"

Lorenzo added as he continued.

"These paintings represent the truth about the spirit world, and some visions are very real. If you see with your own eyes the Apocalypse angel, you will not survive for much longer."

Rogelio remained skeptical as Jesus continued. "Some say that Francisco and Pablo had a connection because of all of this, yet Pablo seemed to have vanished by 1825. Some believed he died some strange death that local authorities kept quiet about. Francisco seemed to distance himself from that period and spoke little of it to friends until his death."

There was a long pause before Rogelio spoke. This was a lot to process.

"Thank you, Señor Moreno, and Señor De Leon for discussing this," was all he could say.

Jesus got up to escort Lorenzo out, "Well my friend, just think about this."

It took another half hour of light conversations and salutations before the old man left, and once he was away, Jesus looked at Rogelio with concern and a glimpse of compassion.

"So, you will stay for another day or two?"

"Yes, to gather my thoughts and take notes."

"Lorenzo is an interesting man, no?"

Rogelio gave him a nod as Jesus collected his bag.

"I will check in with you, Señor, tomorrow."

Moments later, Jesus left. Leaving Rogelio with the quiet of the villa, and a lot to ponder. He had covered up the painting and prepared to go to sleep. As tired as he was the meeting left him unsettled. While he was given some answers, it didn't leave him any comfort. He was tempted to review his lithographs but decided against it. He didn't want to dwell on this and assumed he could have a clearer mind about it the following morning.

He didn't want to admit that Lorenzo's points made sense, in a strange way. Goya had become a recluse in the last twenty years of his life, to various degrees. Was the painter hiding away from forces beyond the ghosts of his memories? Would any of us not be discrete if we felt the threat of malevolent spirits were always ready to seek us out? Or was Goya simply suffering from a mental illness that drove him into hiding? Regardless of if it was spiritual or psychological, did it even matter?

Rogelio left one light on as he took off his clothes, climbed into bed, and turned out the light.

The following morning, the sunlight awoke Rogelio. It seemed like it was going to be a warm day. His mind was still unsettled, but after he showered, got dressed, and walked over to a nearby café for a light breakfast, he felt like he could clear his thoughts, and for a brief time, he still felt the same way he did feel several days earlier, ignorant about the deeper truths about the world. He spoke to a woman in her fifties who had been a native of the area. When she learned which villa he was staying in, she shared some rumored details of whom had stayed there.

"That villa is filled with a lot of memories," she responded, "Some would say the villa is haunted by them."

"Have you ever met Señor Moreno?" Rogelio quizzed the woman.

She gave him a dark glance before she answered. "He comes and goes. The local children are frightened of him. Señor, I would finish your business and be off as soon as you can."

He nodded as he inquired: "Have you ever met Señor De Leon?"

The old woman looked puzzled and clearly didn't know anything about him as she shook her head 'no.' Then the woman drew her hand into her pocket and pulled out a necklace. The wise woman was about to give it to her cousin, but she handed it to him. It was a likeness of Saint Christopher, the Patron Saint of travelers.

"Please keep this for tonight. He'll protect you wherever you go."

Rogelio accepted the gesture, but he had not been devoted since he was a teenager. Yet he felt some comfort as he headed back to the villa. Spending an hour taking note, he unveiled the painting and started to study it. With the limited access, there wasn't much he could do, having nothing to conduct a proper analysis to verify the age of the painting. It was guess work. There was the issue of its condition, which seemed good. If it was a forgery, or another copy, it was a good job.

He found himself studying his lithographs again. The sequence of events didn't make enough sense to him. Goya started his Disasters of War prints around 1810 yet this was painted in 1801. Why didn't Pedro's influence creep up in his other work? *Maybe it did*, he thought. *Maybe it was just unforeseen*. The muse and indirect influences were often hard to define, the way they bleed into one another.

Rogelio found himself getting drowsy by noon and decided to take a nap. He awoke around two o'clock, feeling unusually rested. Rogelio got up and looked out the patio, the town seemed tranquil with people going on with their daily lives. The young man went back into the kitchen and collected some cheese and fruit. A half-hour later he felt a strange sensation. He walked out into the patio and had to blink twice. The landscape had changed: there was a narrow mountain. The tiny outline of a dog crawled up the mountain. He picked up some binoculars to verify what he was seeing. It was like the 1819 painting, *The Dog*.

As he scoured the horizon, he saw a group of tiny figures, men from the 1700s, who were buried as a group, or perhaps a collection of severed heads, like in *Heads in a Landscape*. There also stood a small city with a domed complex. Two robed boys flew over the land, such as in *Fantastic Vision*. Then the vision faded, he blinked and he was facing the same quiet landscape. He stepped back and almost fell onto a bench in the patio, wildly perspiring.

His interest in the subject must have been getting to him. These were signs of an active imagination. He must step back from this situation. He decided to take a walk in the streets of the township and glance through the marketplace. It was helpful. It gave him a moment of normalcy before he headed back to the villa around half-past three. He reviewed his work again until about quarter-past four, when an unexpected change of light in the patio caught his eye. There was another change in the landscape beside a mountain range, he could see two men in a sword fight, such as the painting, "*Fight with Cudgels*". To his left, he could see a succession of old men, shrouded. One man was tailed by a demon. Further right he could see a witches Sabbath, with depictions of the lord of demons in the distance. He saw a succession of ancient robed people, along the edge of a mountain like in the *procession of the holy office*. The moment seemed to represent a great deal of turmoil. Once the visages vanished, and he found himself facing the regular landscape once again.

Rogelio was certain his imagination had overtaken him. There could not be any paranormal phenomenon that was tied to what he was seeing. Could it be a lack of nourishment or lack of sleep? Some of the odder aspects of Goya's life had nothing to do with the afterlife. He had been a man who suffered from misfortune and mental illness.

By now, it was half-past five as he walked back to the square and had some pasta, a sautéed chicken which was delicious, and a mixed salad, then afterwards some fruit. He figured he deserved something special as he rarely indulged himself. He found himself curious as to why Jesus had not called in as of yet to see how he was doing. And he still wondered about the old man.

He started to walk back to the villa, and while looking at the horizon, he shivered. A colossal woman leaned against a mountain hillside beside a temple or a hanging garden, like in the *Leocadia* painting. Then with a blink of an eye it was gone. He dropped to his knees with a dizzy sensation. *Maybe I should leave this place*, he thought. *Can I even get through the night?*

He arrived at the villa with trepidation as well as slight indigestion and lay down. He awoke by eight o'clock. The incident of the walk back had diminished from his memory. Rogelio stood out on the balcony. The night air felt fresh and cool, and he decided he would leave tomorrow morning, even if Jesus was upset over the early departure.

Then he pondered an odd idea. Could Jesus have spiked his food or drink at the villa with some hallucinogen? Was all of this some elaborate set up? If so, what would be the purpose? This notion seemed flimsy, but he decided to inspect the rooms to see if he found anything odd, hidden cameras or audio microphones. He checked the walls and behind the framed pictures he found nothing. Then planter boxes. When he examined the wines, he found no odd fragrances or signs of foul play, and this inspection comforted him even less rather than the fear that he was simply being driven into madness. He found himself lying down and dozing off at around ten.

He awoke forty-five minutes later, all of his senses heightened. He could smell the rosemary and bluebells, and it reminded him of his visits to Mexico as a child to see his great grandmother. It was a time when he was content, and the world was simple. He could see greater details in the night horizon, and even the touch of furniture, the armchair, and the table, seemed more real and intense.

Rogelio stepped out onto the balcony, to the East large groups of people leaving some city, a procession of tormented faces, like in the *Pilgrimage to San Isidro*, and just above them in the sky, a group of robed figures heading towards a river, *Atropos, The Fates*. To his left a ghoul devoured a male from the *Saturn Devouring His Children* painting. There was other carnage, innocent men in a firing squad like in *The Third of May*. The landscape changed again. A village protected by hills and typical of the eighteenth century as he had studied from his history. Thus came a great sound, thunderous thuds, and the earth below him shook. This felt like no illusion as he continued to stare out at the vistas before him. He saw the crown of a head appear in the distance, rising to reveal a naked man, a colossus. Rogelio could hear shrieks and mutterings from the masses in the village below as it seemed to take steps towards the village, then stopped and turned away. It was from the very painting itself. Then the apparitions vanished, and Rogelio had to stop and collect himself.

He stood up and walked over to the painting and unshed it again. He had no doubts now that these visions were not just of the mind, but physical events. Had there been a mere earthquake? Had the neighboring community noticed it? If that had not been the case, then he had entered some parallel realm, some breach between time and space? Perhaps that was the whole point of the 'spirit world' that it was a mere breach. Was this what Pedro had seen? Was it a glimpse into other dimensions? Did he pay a price for such gifts, and did Francisco Goya pay a price for being the mere interpreter? No wonder then why Goya had become so discreet in his final years spent in Bordeaux. Was he hiding from figurative demons or real ones?

Another strange sensation came over Rogelio. He walked towards the balcony, took out the necklace of Saint Christopher, wound his arm and threw it over into the bushes. He pondered a notion at that moment that if God existed, he was absent from here. He could not grasp where this apotheosis came from as he turned and walked back inside.

He moved closer to the painting and caressed the frame. A quiet resignation that came over Rogelio now, an insight, an understanding - When you see the end of one century you cannot see what will come later, and he reasoned that this meant that each century would seem apocalyptic. Perhaps there were truths we were not meant to unveil, and perhaps the modern age was not ready to accept the wisdom of a century before. It didn't leave him with much comfort, just insight, but he felt tired again and needed to sleep, and he didn't care if he ever awoke again as he lied down.

Rogelio awoke at around half-past twelve to a strange cold breeze. He got up and sauntered towards the balcony. Now the landscape was a barren wasteland of mountains and hills, and figures rose from the Earth. Their features were not discernible, but they grew in legion, and Rogelio realized they weren't corporeal but spirits. In the great distance he saw two massive figures that loomed over the legion. Robed with either long hair or hoods, and horns, he could only make out the framework of a face, as the features were ghastly and yet not defined. It was the very painting coming to life, and Rogelio was quickly filled with dread as the figures loomed closer towards him.

He felt the room chill, and he felt shivers down his spine, which he initially didn't discern between his feelings of dread and the physical changes in the room. The figures grew closer, now they were less than a mile away, Rogelio found himself frozen in place. The temperature continued to drop as his breath steamed with every exhale; he was perspiring, and he felt his heart begin to race.

The figures seemed to obscure the legion of spirits he had witnessed as they moved ever closer to him. One of them raised a formless arm at Rogelio, Ice droplets formed around the furniture. The wood of the villa started to creak. His heart continued to race out of his chest. His breathing was labored as the figures seemed to shrink in size as they grew closer. His eyes dilated and widened with his mouth agape, as the figures drew closer and closer, until there was nothing left but blackness.

The next morning Rogelio's body was found by a local servant. The scene was unsettling as Rogelio's face was expressionless, eyes were wide open, he on his back, but his outstretched arms were on their sides. In spite of the arbitrary scene, locals believed he witnessed something terrible. When the local police arrived and investigated the scene, there was no forced entry. No evidence at all that anyone had been there. There was a dampness to the rooms and the furniture, and there seemed to be some mysterious residue at the edge of the balcony, but that was all they found.

They did find his notes and contact book, yet when they reached out to Jesus De Leon, he was nowhere to be found. Even though locals could verify that the old man Lorenzo Moreno had been seen in the area, he could not be found. Some assumed Lorenzo had drifted away into another town. The painting itself was found covered up and retrieved by another collector where it was discovered six months later and announced to the world as a lost work.

The coroner labeled Rogelio's death as a massive coronary. No one would ask any more questions about the incident, and the Spanish authorities felt it was best not to dig any deeper. Some things are best left unexamined. The woman from the town who had spoken to Rogelio would be the only one to hold a candle vigil every year on the anniversary of Rogelio's death for the next twenty years until she passed on. There would always be quiet whispers from the locals about what happened in that villa, how could they not?

*Special Thanks to Eric Mills and Mercedes Sanchez. Thank you to Willie Guerrero.

The Wonder of Inviting a Demon

N. A. Battaglia

Stepping out of a coffee shop and starting down the city block to work, Franklin Stone wondered what it would be like to fight off a demon.

Not in a physical sense, wielding swords and shields, but in an exercise of cognitive fortitude—to starve off an attempted possession just to see if he could do it, to see if he could be unlike the others who failed by yielding to a demon's infestation—a battle of the mind. He wondered how hard it could really be.

After all, his steadfast faith nourished his mind, and he wore a proud, golden chain dangling a cross over his heart. Each step he took he could feel it bounce under his clothing. Coupled with his powerful morals, Franklin knew he bore an impenetrable aegis around his inner soul that no demon could pierce. How could a shapeless entity with no scientific proof govern the innermost mechanisms controlling his brain anyway? How could it coerce and demand his soul forever?

It cannot—it simply cannot, he told himself.

But he still wondered how tantalizing it would be to allow a demon to try anyway. *To tempt fate.* He wished to parry the creature's trickery with games of his own, creating a labyrinth of misdirection through his psyche only to purge the demon when he became bored and disinterested. It would be a herculean task for any demon to win when Franklin carried the home field advantage of his own mind. Fighting a demon would be the epitome of big game hunting, with every advantage to him.

So why not try? he thought.

As if batting against an invisible enemy weren't enough of a thrill and rush, Franklin wondered further about the utility and convenience of such a rivalry. He kept imaging how a demon could help do his bidding before he evicted the unholy occupant from his mind. Indeed, a demon could insulate him from all wrongdoing that transpired. He thought of the visitor as a condom for his soul—lubricating his gears to act out against those who wronged him yet insulating him from any future ramifications for his actions.

Franklin savored at the prospect, remembering particularly when the police would not do anything after he caught his disabled mother's housekeeper stealing money from her.

"Fire her," they scolded him, reminding him the district attorney would not prosecute small-time criminals in an election year. Franklin translated their reminder to mean the district attorney would not prosecute his voters.

He remembered, too, when he and an old co-worker had been engaged in a frustrating, passive-aggressive war that no good supervisor would have entertained. Wouldn't it be convenient for an unavoidable workplace accident to end their quarrel peacefully? Instead, his co-worker got a promotion and was relocated, essentially rewarded for insolence.

As Franklin conjured up new ways to seek retribution, another jerk presented himself. This one bumped into Franklin on the sidewalk without apology or even a recognition of his misconduct. Despite walking on the right side, Franklin fell prey to another stereotypical New York City denizen power-walking the wrong way and refused to compromise the space. The unfriendly impact rocked the arm holding Franklin's coffee, splashing it on his wrist and across the cuff of his white shirt. Without breaking stride, the social miscreant strode away without any ramifications—blissful impunity for the depraved.

For now, Franklin thought. As he turned back to look incredulously at the man, another person struck Franklin's other arm. "Watch where you are going!" the friendly commuter reminded him.

It was just another endorsement for Franklin's industrious desire for a demon to exact revenge for him. Franklin debated why he even continued to wonder anymore. He should just challenge the first demon he could find who lusted for possession, then reap the benefits and banish the demon back to hell—all as a simple exercise of mental calisthenics.

He continued across the street, walking with the traffic light but earning the honks of several officious taxis yearning to turn right on red—albeit illegally. He shot glares at each of them, backed with no more power than his sullen eyes. His frustrated eyes. The taxi drivers could see it too but the honking continued unabated.

Why wait any longer?

Franklin arrived at work, entering into a lobby where he was greeted by others congregating.

"Good morning, Father Stone," one elderly woman greeted him.

"And the same to you, Helen," Franklin replied with an engaging and friendly smile, cloaking what he was still writhing over from his excursion down a typical New York City block and into the church.

As he pushed through the doors of the vestibule, formally known as the narthex of the church, another gentleman greeted him with a smile and a bow of the head, which Franklin ceremoniously returned. He continued along the side aisle into the sacristy, closing the door behind him with a swift slam and the confirming click of the hinge.

He took off his jacket, hanging it up on the nearest hook before pivoting to set his coffee on the counter. He was reminded of the dark coffee stain on his white shirt. Later efforts to wash the stain would only fade the dark patch, not dispelling it as completely as he hoped. *Damn people.*

He sat down in his chair, observing a flurry of blinking voicemails and a forest of sticky notes planted across his desktop.

Sitting there, paralyzed as to how to triage his duties and obligations as deputized by the Holy Church, Father Franklin Stone again found himself wondering if he could manage a demon trying to possess him. He was not like the others. He was indoctrinated through Christ, protected by the Father, Son, and the Holy Spirit, which was exactly why he couldn't take certain matters into his own hands without a demon's assistance.

The tabloids would read: *Priest Stabs Housekeeper, Exposes Corrupt District Attorney, and Pummels J-walking Jerk-off, All Before 9 AM Mass.*

He sighed to himself and stood up, surveying the counter for his coffee and walking over to retrieve it.

What would a demon sound like?

What would it say to me?

Franklin wondered as he finished his coffee, tossing the cup into the trash and not the recycling. It wasn't a recycling type of morning.

He wondered how he could even provoke a demon to try to lay claim to his soul in the first place. *Would I have to do something evil?* Franklin wondered. *Would I have to call upon Satan himself?*

Shaking his head, he walked back over to his desk, sitting back down to stare at the blinking red button on his phone indicating his unplayed voicemails. The light was bright red like an evil eye in the dark, or blood spilled from a beast's fresh kill.

Franklin stared at the light, shifting his mind from his obligations to an invitation. *Come get me,* he thought. "Come to me, try to command what is not yours," he said aloud, "I'm here, ready, and willing."

He sat there for a moment, feeling nothing more than embarrassment for speaking aloud such sacrilegious things in a church. He paused, embarrassed, then considered how he felt.

Nothing yet, he whispered to himself.

Perhaps he was too hardened of a target. Maybe a demon would not think to attack a priest, let alone in a church. On the other hand, what a prize he would be to the most insatiable of demons! Was he not a cherished target among evil, to be a pawn of darkness?

Franklin reached around his neck and withdrew the chain carrying the golden cross over his chest. *Maybe this will make it easier for you,* Franklin considered. *More appetizing.*

But nothing happened.

In depredation of his holy obligations, he held several masses without wearing the cross he left in his desk. The words he spoke, settling over the mass goers, carried little emphasis to convey any true holy power behind them. He spoke flat as an out-of-tune piano, his words as dead as firewood waiting to be burned to ash.

Franklin fulfilled his priestly obligations in rote fashion until it was time to leave, when he tucked his cross deeper into his desk drawer to hide it from wandering eyes—behind the box of paperclips, quite the inappropriate place for a holy symbol bestowed to a priest. He didn't care. Franklin wondered if it really would matter where it was stored.

He exited the sacristy, walking down the center nave of the church to leave. Congregants and others wished him a good evening, but he didn't recognize any of the actual words they muttered to him. He was only able to fire back a half smile and nod. He sighed of relief as he made it to the door, pushing it open and diving outside as if he was a fish out of water yearning for new ocean realty.

The air outside was crisp, reminding him of his jacket hanging inside. He was not willing to double back through his congregants and repeat another round of smiles from his crumbling face and failing expression.

Franklin decided he'd take the long way home, turning to the right and continuing to walk. He continued wondering whether or not he would get his wish, whether a demon really would attempt governance of a priest, even if just for a short time.

Franklin couldn't imagine what it would be like, he was intoxicated by the very thought of fighting off evil with just his mind. Under this influence, he bumped into another pedestrian, this time not baptizing his clothing with coffee but returning the favor to another person.

"Excuse me!" a voice stirred behind him, "How about sorry, asshole!" the woman shrieked.

Franklin kept going without turning around. It was best to not let her or anyone else catch a glimpse of his face and recognize him. He smirked to himself. He could hear a continued commotion behind him, but he didn't care.

Is this how it will feel when I'm possessed? he wondered. *Will this be what it's like battling a demon? Is this how others feel each day?*

A myriad of scenarios ran through Franklin's mind as he considered how it would feel to make first contact. Would it be obvious? He wondered how he'd prepare and what traps he should begin to lay as a vanguard to his mind.

It was becoming dusk now, Franklin realized after being distracted with his thoughts on his long march. He should probably head back in the direction of home. *All just to rest up and replicate another torturous day tomorrow, and the next, for all perpetuity.*

He came to a bridge overlooking a majestic river just in time to catch the sunset. He stared out at the pinks, oranges, and yellows burning across the sky, reflected in the divinity of the clouds glaring back at him. *How pretty*, he mused. *There's such beauty in nature when man is removed.*

Looking down, he could see the mirror of the sky on the water's surface, promising him a better disposition for tomorrow. "Red sky at night, sailor's delight. Red sky in morning, sailors take warning," Franklin rhymed in a juvenile tune, ending with an overly-exaggerated smile.

His smile kept curling up, pinching his cheeks with glee, the red and orange hues of the water's surface growing commensurate with his smile.

As the reflection grew brighter and brighter, it was then, and only then, that Franklin wondered no more. He lost his battle with a demon.

Calm Waters

Rachel Unger

Winter, 1804

My dear Captain Croft,

I am settled in now at Deal, uncertain of when we will next speak. Well, letters have done for us before, and I will do my best to keep you apprised of matters involving the household. At present I have taken some rooms on the shore, near the barracks and Deal Castle. I was advised that this was a very desirable place for the wife of a naval officer to stay. I have indeed observed that there are some two or three other women here who seem to harbour no good will for the sea. One such, Mrs. Matthews, has lodging close by. Her husband is a midshipman on the newly commissioned *Hawk* out of Plymouth. She is congenial company.

I would, of course, rather yours – it is a strange thing to suddenly be without you. It is stranger still to find myself a shore wife, and one mourning the loss of our baby. On that topic I still doubt that I am much safer on dry land, my dear, though you were rather insistent. I know we agreed we would not discuss it further, but I find myself sometimes at a loss, listening to the empty air here, waiting for... but it is no matter.

It is merely the odd architecture of a new place. You know how I am always disordered, the first twenty-four hours or so in a new berth. And perhaps there will be a child, one day.

I have engaged a Mrs. Hawthorne to look after the cooking and cleaning, though I would guess it was the shortest interview in the history of such things. Not a woman of many words, is my Mrs. Hawthorne. I find this is true of many of those who were born and still live in Deal. They often seem preoccupied and wary of the rest of us – no doubt concerned with what Napoleon's antics in France will mean for them here.

Speaking of our adversary, I have heard that we can see Calais from here on a clear day. However, since my arrival France appears to be hiding from us. There is nothing outside our windows other than rain and mist. At times, the masts of the ships in the Downs are visible, but mostly it is just fog, the gleam of water on the cobblestones, and the houses huddled together against the voiceless damp. Sometimes even the fire burns quietly, daring not a pop or crackle.

I can hear the sea from the house at all hours, and yet the timbers and furniture do not sway along with it the way they have these last five years. I confess that I miss it. However, I am determined to adjust to these new circumstances.

If the weather clears, I will walk to the Navy Yard and see the Downs for myself. I will take this unease from the house and leave it on the sand so it can trouble me no more.

Yours in affection,

Sophia

Dearest Captain Croft,

It is still too early for a letter from you, but I have been to the Downs as I said I would in my last missive. I want to send my impressions – not before they fade, as I consider it unlikely for them to do so, but to beseech your opinion of the events.

The weather continued to hold poor, but I could not condone another day spent entirely inside. The wind had taken to shrieking past the windows in a way that was very disconcerting. I would have thought it the voice of an unhappy child, yet I know there are none on this street. When I asked, Mrs. Hawthorne told me she had learnt to ignore it, but I felt myself practically driven from the house. I armed myself with an umbrella and my stout wool coat, and I set out to see the ships. I was determined that if I could not have you, my dear Captain, then I would have a tangible reminder of these happy years I have spent in your company on the deck of a ship.

The Downs are unlike any harbour I have seen, and I suspect would also hold unique in your view. They exist as a calm anchorage between Deal Castle and the Goodwin Sands offshore, reached only by tender or rowboats. I had thought to see proud and noble ships under repair or awaiting resupply. I had expected perhaps some of the twenty-nine ships said to make up the Downs Squadron of the North Sea Fleet.

I did not expect to see derelict hulls and vessels that were visibly unfit to sail. Perhaps one ship in five seemed worthy of being afloat, and the rest… Seeing the gaping holes, some barely tarred, some with tar leaking down the side as though from a wound… And no one, not a soul on the beach. Nor was anyone onboard from what I could see. There were no colors flying on any of the ships, and in the dull press of the fog the masts looked like nothing more than the discarded bones of some ancient beast.

I cannot even now convey to you what the sight did to freeze my heart. The splintered wood, so like the limbs of that creature we saw a month ago...

In an instant, my mind cast back to seeing it climbing over the port side in the moonlight. For a moment I could almost smell that sharp, burnt odour again. I know you think there is nothing to be gained by going over those moments, but I will speak of it! I remember it turning to us and making that awful whistling noise – if not for Lieutenant Ashton having the watch, I think it would have killed us both that night. I remember the words he spoke, how it stabbed at him in fury...

How my abdomen flared with agony, and I knew our child was no more.

And it was in this moment of recollection that someone grasped my arm, appearing without warning like a wraith out of the mist. As he shook me I recoiled, and he shouted something I did not understand. In my confusion, I could only stare at him until I recognized his clothes – they were the kind of garments issued to any ship's crew. I confess to no small measure of relief.

I am, as you know, George, well used to sailors. At first, I thought his demeanor no worse than that of others I have known when they have had a bit of a tipple.

"It comes for you!" he bellowed. His breath was wet and rank with more than liquor. "Now you have seen them it will seek you out, and it will feast on marrow and meat as you scream – " The rags he wore fell back from his arm as he reached for me once more, and his bones stood out from his flesh like a breakwater. The thinness of it was shocking and too familiar, too much like...

I backed away and the cobblestones favored my feet more

than his, for he fell. I seized upon this chance and fled, making my way back to my rooms with no little speed. The wind followed me, bringing with it his imprecations far longer than I would have expected the sound to carry.

That wind howled around the house continually for the remainder of the day. I know this can only be a capricious bit of weather. I know what he said was only the effect of drink and malnutrition. And yet... even Mrs. Hawthorne peered warily out the windows as evening slunk in. Sleep came fitfully when it came at all. I have been leaping at every window-rattle, and I find myself now writing this braced with a strong cup of tea. Sunrise is but a dim light only now bringing the stormy world outside my window into focus.

I do not know what to make of his... his accusations. He cannot have known about what we saw, about that thing the lieutenant drove off. Can he? Can word have spread amongst the crew? I was so beset with the loss of our baby after, I had little thought for else.

Write me with all possible haste, I beg you. Tell me you are well and have fair winds, that the weather plagues only here. Tell me that you haven't seen... Write me, my dear Captain, and it will be as though you were here and all is well.

I count on your reply,

Sophia

Dear George,

I can scarce believe that you of all people should give credit to the foolish idea that I am some sort of delicate creature, prone to imagining things! The sailor at the Downs was <u>not</u> the production of an agitated mind, and the only <u>projection</u>

occurring was in the loudness of his voice. (What the workings of his mind were to produce such words, I cannot guess.)

Now that you have been disabused of this notion (for you most assuredly have), let us return to more practical discourse. I have spent several amusing afternoons trading stories with Mrs. Matthews. (She particularly liked the one about the seagull in Lisbon – your hat was never the same again, was it?) She has had a letter from her husband containing news from Boulogne. His indications of the number of French ships and troops along the coast are far greater than I had expected. Mrs. Matthews and I are agreed, as I expect you are, that the new alliance with Sweden will send a strong message to Napoleon that the might of the British Navy is not to be underestimated.

Your recounting of the recent engagement with French ships only encourages my hopes in this regard, and I am glad to hear that Lieutenant Ashton is recovering the use of his hand. I only wish I were there to see it with you. Please pass along my encouragement to him…

As I wrote that last line, George, I had a surprise visitor – Mrs. Matthews came to insist on my presence at supper tomorrow. "We shall spend a merry evening," she told me when she came with the invitation. She reached out to clasp my hand with fingers that could have been made of ice, but her cheeks burned bright. "My girl has obtained a roast – a beef roast, if you please! I own that not even the Prime Minister will have a meal of such quality."

I squeezed her fingers and said, "I wager that is not all that's been delivered," and she laughed. The happy sound of it danced around the room and lifted my heart.

"You're right, of course – a misdirected letter from my Henry arrived today. He is to resupply here in only a few weeks!

There is even talk of some shore leave." She fair glowed with the news. "Now, promise me you'll come."

I did so and she slipped out the door into a veritable gale. Mrs. Hawthorne came to stand beside me at the window, scowling at the rain-lashed cobbles.

"Hopefully this storm will wash through before tomorrow night," she grumbled. I was touched by her concern until she continued, "It's not wise to venture out in this sort of weather – more than one man's been lost in such things, particularly if he's fool enough to go out at night." Her look then was direct and – as I am not a fool – I promised I would send my regrets if the weather worsened. Mrs. Hawthorne jerked her chin in a nod of sorts and vanished back into the kitchen.

Keep yourself well and be sure to wrap up against the chill. It would not do to have a Captain giving away the British fleet with an ill-timed sneeze. I trust that the matter of my own health is now settled as well.

Unless you meant the entire preceding letter as some sort of elaborate joke, by which I was not amused in the least.

Yours in affection, though you may not deserve it,
Sophia

George, oh George, I hardly know where to begin.

I went to supper with Mrs. Matthews, as I told you in my last letter. I wore my warmest dress, for lately it is impossible to keep a room heated. The night was quiet, for once, the storms blown out to sea for the first time in I cannot remember how long. Mrs. Matthews's cook produced a roast quite as good as any other I have eaten, and we talked until quite late.

I said I was quite capable of walking home, given that her

rooms are separated from mine only by a handful of houses. Mrs. Matthews was in such high spirits that she laughed and said she would accompany me, it being so clear and calm.

We saw no one else along the road at that late hour. And then... we came to a place where there was... there came the smell of a lightning strike. A lightning strike on a clear night, but thick as though lightning had struck the same place over, and over, and over again. You know that smell, George. It was the smell of that thing that hauled itself over the side of the boat that night. With no little unease, I cast about to find the source.

Even as the purulent moon glared down, the creature emerged from the darkness of the water. It was the same as before and I will speak of it, George! It had the same arm-like limbs, ending in points rather than hands, and how such a thing could swim I do not know.

It came up the beach towards us, the same glistening yellow-white as the ghoulish moon, with my breath stopped up in my throat as surely as water held back by a dam. I could only watch it come, so otherworldly that I could not act on any notion of fleeing or even reacting. It was nearly upon us when Mrs. Matthews screamed.

In reflex, I found myself repeating the words that Lieutenant Ashton had spoken, in the hope that I could also drive the creature away from us.

It recoiled from me on hearing those words. Then it stabbed at me with one appendage, and I tried to step back. The sharp point of it pierced my forearm as I moved, and it held me fast.

I had never imagined such pain could exist. The creature shook me, the way the sailor had, and through the shock and nearly mindless hurt the words came out of me again.

Every time I spoke the words the creature retreated a little more, dragging me with it. I do not know which was worse – the agony of my arm, wrenched without ceasing, or the terror as we came closer and closer to the water. I kept saying those words, because each repetition diminished the thing. Finally, shouting, I struck out at the head of the creature, and it shuddered so hard that my arm came free of its blade. I retreated, never taking my eyes off it.

The pointed limbs came up as though trying to cover its ears, but the withering continued. By the time the creature collapsed onto the beach, it had shrunk to mere shreds of skin. The next wave slapped at the remains, nearly tearing them in half. Within moments, the creature had been reduced to sea foam that one might see on any shoreline. Salt spray glistened on my damp, heavy skirts and the horror of my near escape made me shudder.

I clutched my gory arm and turned to find Mrs. Matthews fainted dead away on the street. I ran to the house, pounding until Mrs. Hawthorne opened the door. I do not know why no one else came, given Mrs. Matthews's scream and my own shouting.

Mrs. Hawthorne took charge, striding to the next house and hammering on their door. "Every soul on this street is awake, so there's no use in pretending!" No one could have slept through her pronouncement, so it wasn't a surprise to see the front curtain move. "It's dead," Mrs. Hawthorne insisted. "A good Christian would open up and lend aid now that the danger has passed. You claim it loudly enough, Catherine, now comes time for proof." The door cracked open to reveal a wary face and Mrs. Hawthorne shoved the gap wider. "Send that young boy of yours for the doctor. The missus may have a head injury. Get a coat and help me get her back home." The two of them carried Mrs. Matthews between them, as matter of fact as you please. I trailed behind like some kind of spirit, feeling nearly insubstantial in comparison to their doughtiness.

Mrs. Hawthorne repeated the vehement knocking and piercing tone at Mrs. Matthews' door and to much the same effect. We walked home before the doctor arrived. If my arm had not been bleeding, it would have been hard to believe the night had ever held monsters.

Mrs. Hawthorne took care of me herself, cleaning my wound and bandaging it, finding the mundane in the moment by advising me to "soak that dress immediately, or you'll never get the blood out." I have never been so grateful for someone to remember the needs of mere laundry.

My head rang, though the house was astonishingly quiet. She had some more advice for me afterwards.

"There now," Mrs. Hawthorne said with a hard look, "why don't you write a letter to that Captain of yours – get it all out of your head so you can see it plain. You'll not want to sleep until you have, trust you me." And it seemed such good advice, so calm and reasonable that so I have done, and I find myself now almost unbearably weary.

My dear Captain, it is now nearly two days later – I did sleep, though I didn't expect to do so. I woke to sweltering heat and the last ray of light slinking back over the windowsill like a sneak thief, taking the day with it. My arm had swollen to nearly twice the size overnight, and I was near dizzy with fever.

Mrs. Hawthorne seemed to expect this, for she was sitting in my room watching over me. She helped me dress and make my way to the kitchen, where I roamed with a restless unease while she prepared supper.

I could not settle, only clutch my pulsing arm and then release it, even more unsettled. We ate together in the kitchen, though I did little more than pick at my food. Mrs. Hawthorne did not appear to mind the company, silent though I was.

It was after dark when my arm spasmed. It felt like something moving inside, rather than the motion coming from my own body. I tore at the bandage, discovering to my horror that I was right. Something twisted in the wound, causing fresh jolts of pain with its every motion. Mrs. Hawthorne seized a goodly-sized kitchen knife but hesitated, watching me for some sign of... of I know not what.

Then the thing forced its way out of me, even as I screamed. It slid free of my body, dropping to the kitchen floor where it lay as though stunned. Seeing it, I could scarcely credit my senses. It resembled a tiny, wax-like doll, arms and legs drawn close to its body and little toes curled in. I crouched at once, concerned it had hurt itself in the fall. My blood had streaked its body a kind of pink in the lamplight. I marveled at how like an infant it was except for its size – cradling it in my hand, I found it smaller than a kitten. It made a mewling noise, twitching its slender, sinewy form. It was nearly the size of my palm, and I had a moment of astonishment that it had grown so much inside of me.

But then it stretched again, and I saw its arms ended in the same needle-like appendages as the monster on the beach the previous night. The illusion of it being a child dissipated like mist before the sun, and I was filled with fury. That it should dare to look like a baby – when one of them had taken our baby – I could not bear it.

I would like to say that I did not know myself in that moment, but I cannot lie to you. I will not. I seized the creature and I understood what I was doing. It thrashed in my grip as my fingers tightened, and it made one last moan before I began to strangle it.

It tried to get free, jerking and twisting. The force of it jarred my wound and I cried out. I could see Mrs. Hawthorne keeping the knife ready in her hand. The creature's motions were so strong for something so tiny, but I knew I could not let it get away. In desperation I brought my hands down at the edge of the sink as hard as I could, even as I squeezed my fingers tight against its throat. I could feel the impact vibrate through the creature as its head hit the slate.

Finally, it stopped moving. Gasping, I leaned against the sink myself. I opened my hand to see it lying, tiny and still in my grasp. It had been dead nearly as long as it had been alive, and I had been instrumental in both conditions. These things were clear and also incomprehensible to me. I was fury and despair both. That monster had given me a second baby – and I had killed it.

"What do we do with it?" I asked Mrs. Hawthorne, not expecting her to know any more than I did.

"Cut off the head," she said promptly, "and then we'll have to bury it inland, so it can't come back."

I do not know how she knew this, but I handed over the creature. I could not watch her do it, and the sound of the knife thudding into the counter conveyed the events almost more than I could stand. Afterwards, she found a jar and I placed the pieces inside. She cleaned out my wound again, and I saw how much bigger the opening was than it had been the night before. Only then did I wonder if Lieutenant Ashton had lain abed with fever as I had, if he had dealt with his own tiny creature alone.

Mrs. Hawthorne patted my shoulder with a kind of warmth and approval that I had not previously seen from her. "It will heal cleanly now, I'm sure," she said, and bid me rest in the kitchen for a moment. She returned with a simple cart and pony.

She drove us through the night, with the sky beginning to let fall some rain and mist rising from the ground to greet it. It was just light when we stopped in Eythorne. Mrs. Hawthorn led the way past the Baptist cemetery, tugging on my uninjured arm to bring me to the back of a chapel newly built. We buried the creature there, taking turns digging some few feet deep. It was… not a task I should like to attempt again. The hour or the weather must have kept the minister indoors, for none interrupted our eerie work.

And then we returned to Deal, though I scarce remember much of that journey. I sit here now at the kitchen table, staring at my earlier letter to you where it sits on the mantel.

I think, George, there can be no possible reason that would seem sufficient to keep me a shore wife after this. It is demonstrably no safer here than with you. I will arrange to pay the yearly taxes and then wait for you to send word where you will make landfall next.

I am also doubling Mrs. Hawthorne's wages. I trust you will not object.

Write soonest and tell me where I may rejoin you. I will brook no opposition on this matter.

With very great affection, your
Sophia

To Lieutenant Ashton, crew of the *Neptune*

Another creature came ashore this week, very like the one you told me of in your last letter. I'd been watching for it, but it was the missus of the household who found it. She had more resolution in her than I expected. She pretty near did the whole job herself, though she was grateful for the doctoring I did afterwards. We buried it up in the churchyard near my Albert, God rest his soul. Holy ground still seems to keep them contained.

I expect we won't see another creature for some months, now. I hope the same holds true for you.

Your sister,

Agatha Hawthorne

To Midshipman Matthews, crew of the *Hawk*

My dear husband,

I must tell you of the strangest dream I had the other night! It was after Sophia came for supper and I took a fall on the cobblestones – which was a minor injury, don't waste a moment on it. The dream is the most disconcerting one I have ever had. It is the effect, no doubt, of the wind, which has begun to howl around the house in the most unpleasant way…

Sarah

Happy Girl Therapy

Koji A. Dae

Five years ago, Greta would have scoffed at the desperate ladies lining up at the RejuveNation doors for lifts and tucks. That was before her hips widened from toting around toddlers and worry creases lined her face from yelling every time Robert or Angela got too close to something dangerous. But thanks to the erasure of all signs of motherhood from her co-worker Monica's face and a stellar referral program, Greta found herself bypassing the waiting room and heading straight through the double doors.

The halls were stark. More clinical than spa-like. Greta lingered in front of door twenty-six and hummed her rules to herself, the tune bouncing through the bare corridor. *No surgery. No injections. Nothing permanent. Just something to feel a little fresher.*

Fresh. Hah. A full night of sleep would probably leave her fresher than anything the spa could offer.

The door swung open and a young man in a white lab coat greeted Greta with a warm smile. "Greta? Right on time. I'm Dr. Macy."

Greta eased into the large office. Despite the plush carpet, it shared the rest of the building's minimalism. The tinted window behind the desk obscured the dark forest beyond. The dim light glinted off a bowl filled with smooth, white stones on the doctor's desk. Two extravagant paintings hung on the walls. One featured a naked girl with long red hair stepping from the sea onto a deserted beach. The other showed a girl with glass slippers ascending into a carriage. Both had perfect skin.

"You enjoy fairy tales?"

Dr. Macy nodded. "Every woman deserves her fairytale. That's why they come to us."

Greta raised her eyebrows. "Are you the evil sea witch or fairy godmother?"

"Neither. Just someone helping you achieve your goals. Sit down, please."

She sank into a plush, lavender chair and sighed. Dr. Macy didn't seem old enough to be a doctor. That was a sign of aging, right? It was one thing to think teens looked too pudgy in the cheeks to drive, but to think a doctor was too young to practice? Next, she'd be sitting on her porch, yelling at kids to stay away from her roses. Except she didn't have time for roses. Or porches.

She didn't tell him that. But she told him about the two births, the hours upon years of childcare, and her desperate need for a vacation.

"Does that make me a horrible mom?" She sipped a glass of cool water, knowing it did.

"Not at all." He beamed, showing perfect teeth. "Especially if you have one of those high-spirited, energetic kids."

"I definitely have one of those. Robert. The older one. He's four now. Boundless energy, super sensitive about everything."

She dug through her purse and took out her phone to show off her wallpaper.

Dr. Macy leaned forward with polite curiosity. "Fine looking children. But parents deserve time to themselves. Unfortunately, especially with single parents, it's not always realistic. Sometimes you have to make do with a solid night of sleep, right?"

She sank deeper into the chair. He understood. "Yes. Even half a night would be wonderful. But Robert has night terrors. His screaming wakes me up two or three times a night."

Dr. Macy sucked his teeth and nodded. "I think you're a perfect candidate for our Happy Girl treatment."

"Happy Girl?" Greta hadn't felt happy in months, and she hadn't been a girl in years.

"We're still working on the name." Dr. Macy winked in a way Greta could almost mistake as flirtatious if she wasn't an aging mother. "It's a cutting edge nanite treatment that repairs overworked neurons while you sleep, leaving you feeling refreshed in the morning."

No surgery. No injections. Nothing permanent. "That sounds intense for me."

"Nanites sound scary." He gave a half laugh and shook his head. "But they are no more invasive than antibiotics or vaccines. You take a pill an hour before bedtime. The nanites hitch into your bloodstream and, while you're asleep, they repair your brain. They die out by morning, and a second pill flushes them from your system. Nothing invasive, nothing permanent. Just a mini-vacation for three nights that will leave you fully refreshed."

Dr. Macy stared unblinking at Greta and waited.

Mesmerized, she almost agreed without thinking. But her

117

lips remained immune to his charms. "Will I be able to wake up if my kids need me? Like I said, Robert has nightmares sometimes."

Sometimes? She couldn't remember not waking and rushing into his room to find him pointing at some ghastly apparition only he could see. She shivered.

"Of course," he assured her. "You may be groggier than normal, but you can wake up. Many mothers who use this treatment tell me their more challenging children are easier to deal with after Happy Girl. It's amazing what a bit of rest can do for all aspects of your life."

The Happy Girl treatment consisted of a blister of six gel caps. Three nightly ones: red, blue, and purple. The morning ones were all milky white. Greta slipped them into her purse, gave the secretary her credit card, and prayed for an easy evening.

***

Bath time spilled over, toothbrushing was rushed, and the bedtime story was cut in half because the children continued to giggle and play. But eventually Greta got Robert and Angela into their bunk beds and their breath calmed to the steady whisper of sleep.

She unclenched her teeth, took a deep breath, and tiptoed out of their room. In the bathroom she popped the red gel cap from the pack. Funny to think it contained active nanotech. No. Not active yet. Dr. Macy had explained her body's electric current would activate them. She swallowed the pill with a large glass of water—for better lubrication—and put herself to bed not feeling any different. If it wasn't for Monica's flawless skin, Greta would have thought it was a scam, preying on the vanity of women. She closed her eyes and tried to remember what waking up refreshed felt like.

***

She woke to bright sunlight streaming through the window. She stretched against the flannel sheets. Her joints popped but her body ached a little less than normal. Her head was foggy, like the slushiness of a hangover without the pounding. Right. The white pill would supposedly lift that. She stumbled to the bathroom. From the mirror, a younger version of herself stared out. She winked and no crow's feet appeared around her eye. Not a miracle, but damn close.

Suppressing laughter, she danced to the kitchen. Her amusement dampened as she was met by three cookie sheets filled with freshly baked gingersnaps.

"What the—"

"Mamma!" Robert burst into the room with heavy raccoon circles beneath his wide eyes. "I called for you and you didn't come!"

She bent down and wrapped her arms around him. He was too young for tired eyes. "Did you have a nightmare?"

He nodded into her shoulder, his face wet. "It was horrible. This old woman came into our room. She asked which of us she should eat first." He shuddered, his words coming faster. "Her eyes were huge, her voice all scratchy."

Greta squeezed harder. Robert didn't usually remember his nightmares, let alone describe them in such detail. "You know it was just a dream, right?"

He sniffed. "Yeah."

"Mommy is taking a medicine that makes her very sleepy. So, I might be harder to wake up. But if you were ever in real danger, I'd come for you."

He gave her a coy half-grin. "Did you make cookies for breakfast?"

Greta eyed the gingersnaps. Sleep baking? Was that a thing? She shrugged. "You can have one. But just one."

Angela toddled around the corner, rubbing sleepy eyes.

"Do you want a cookie?" Greta held out a gingersnap.

Angela shook her head and backed away, as if her own mother frightened her.

Angela had already been frightened of dogs, her daycare teacher, and the mailman. But of her own mother? Greta rolled her eyes, stored the cool cookies in a Tupperware for work, and started preparing oatmeal for breakfast.

"Can I have her cookie?" Robert asked.

"No," Greta sighed. "One's enough."

"That's not fair. I hate oatmeal!" He stomped out of the kitchen.

***

Greta was late for work, but the gingersnaps eased her colleagues' anger.

Settled at her desk, Greta fished Dr. Macy's card from her purse. His personal line in case she had any complications. Did gingersnaps count as a complication?

"Could the nanites cause sleepwalking?"

"Sleepwalking?" His voice held warm concern without the tightness of worry. "Perhaps, but it isn't a common side effect."

"What about, well, sleep baking?"

"Sleep baking?" Greta could imagine the way his eyebrows shot up in amusement.

"I woke up to dozens of cookies on the counter. I don't know where they came from." As she described the problem, a memory played at the edge of her mind: the way she swayed in the kitchen, wearing her robe, mixing dough with a wooden spoon.

120

"There is an issue if you're operating dangerous appliances while you're asleep."

Greta thought of her electric oven. It never held the right temperature and burned almost everything. The gas range top had a faulty pilot light she had to use matches on. She shouldn't be operating it while awake, let alone while sleeping.

"Was baking something you did before? Something you don't have as much time for now?"

Greta remembered the perfectly shaped macarons she brought to parties, back when she still went to parties. "I used to love baking."

"It's possible the nanites recognized baking as a release for you. I wouldn't be too worried about it if it's something you're familiar with. How did you feel this morning? Rested?"

"Yes." She tried not to wrinkle her newly smooth forehead with thought. "Unbelievably so."

Throughout the day Greta's concerns about the cookies faded as her colleagues told her how fresh and young she looked.

"What's your secret?" they asked.

She couldn't admit the truth. "Gingersnaps. They have lots of antioxidants and are so relaxing to bake." Only as she said this did she realize she had never baked gingersnaps before.

***

That evening, bedtime was worse than usual. Angela refused to be tucked in. Robert went willingly into bed but kept biting his chapped lower lip and casting nervous glances at the door. Every time Greta attempted to turn out the lights and leave, he stopped her.

"Mamma, you'll come if I need you?"

"Yes." Greta tried not to groan. "I promise."

Angela remained sitting up and held Mr. Scruffly, her ragged teddy bear, tight to her chest.

"Witch," she hissed, pointing at Greta with a big-girl frown.

Greta rolled her eyes, flicked off the light, and shut the door halfway. She didn't turn back when Robert called for her again. If she answered every call, she'd never get to her own bed.

She swallowed her blue pill and didn't even have enough energy to read a chapter in her book before a dark, dreamless sleep took her. In the morning she slept through two minutes of her alarm's shrill buzz.

She sat up, foggier than the previous morning, and padded to the bathroom for her white pill of clarity.

As she passed her children's room, Robert poked his head around the door.

"Mamma, is it you?" he whispered.

"Of course it's me. Who else would it be?"

He glanced down the hall then stepped from his room. "The witch was here again. She was terrible, Mamma. She stole your face, but it was all wrinkly, and her eyes were red."

Greta dipped down to Robert's level. "That sounds scary, sweetie. But it was just a dream. There's no witch, and no one has stolen my face, see?"

She held his tiny hand to her smooth cheek.

He hesitated, looking in her eyes, then threw his arms around her neck.

In the kitchen gingerbread men, complete with sugar icing and chocolate chip buttons, stared at Greta with sloppy smiles. She gave one to Robert, but Angela wouldn't come out of their room.

"Sure, I may look ten years younger, but I'll also weigh twenty pounds more after this treatment," Greta grumbled as she packed the small men up for work.

***

The girls in the office gobbled up the sugary treats, trusting Greta's lies that the ginger would smooth their complexions and ease their stress. As she gave one to Monica, she thought maybe she wasn't lying. Maybe the heat of the spice helped people remain youthful.

"I know your secret," Monica said, nibbling the head of her man.

"My secret?" Greta lifted her eyebrows and the skin of her face tensed in a lovely way she hadn't felt in years.

"It's not the ginger. You went to RejuveNation."

Greta shrugged. Her shoulders felt light, and she shimmied them back into place. "No use denying it. But our secret, right?"

Monica laughed. "Sure, our secret. What are you on?"

"Happy Girl. The name's ridiculous, but it works. I have one more dose, and I feel like I'll wake up in the body of an eighteen-year-old."

Monica frowned, revealing a few fine wrinkles Greta had missed before. "Isn't Happy Girl that experimental one with the nanites?"

"Experimental? No, they didn't say that." Dr. Macy had mentioned it was new, but not experimental. "It must have passed the final tests." Greta gave her new body a flabless flaunt before heading back to her desk.

***

Strangely energized, Greta powered through her tasks and left the office fifteen minutes early. Maybe enough time to stop at the ice cream parlor and treat the kids to something that wasn't ginger-flavored.

But at daycare pickup, the teacher pulled Greta aside and lowered her voice to a confidential level. "I'm worried about Robert. He slept through snack-time, even when I tried to wake him."

Greta sighed. "He's still having those nightmares."

"I don't want to overstep, but it might be time to consider a psychologist for him." The teacher took Greta's elbow and led her to a desk covered with papers. She rummaged through them and held up a drawing. Greta could make out a hunched figure approaching what could only be the children's bunk bed. The figure wore a pink robe, similar to Greta's. "It's very detailed for a four-year-old."

Greta took the drawing to study it. Her free hand fluttered to her chest, and she bit her lower lip. Why would he put the witch in her bathrobe?

"That's not all." The teacher handed her a second drawing. This one had the hunched figure over Robert's bed, its mouth open in a big oval. Blue lines connected the boy's open mouth to the figures. "I know the nightmares have been going on for some time, but this is new. When I asked him what the pictures were about, he said an old woman comes into his room at night and sucks away his energy. He was adamant it wasn't a dream."

"Not a dream?" Greta eyed the splotch of pink. "What else could it be?"

"It seems like he might have problems separating reality from fiction. A psychologist might help with that."

Greta folded the papers and tucked them into her purse. She tried not to think about the pink robe as she strapped Angela, kicking and yelling, into her car seat.

***

That night she put the kids to bed with no nonsense. Hugs

and kisses for Robert, a frustrated chasing down of Angela, and no story. Despite the energy Happy Girl gave her, she didn't have the patience to deal with their squirming and whining. Not on her fairytale night, when she would turn into a beautiful princess. She was asleep before the pill dissolved.

***

"Mamma! Please, no!"

Greta's eyelids lifted to the disorienting figure of a gingerbread house, the eaves covered with a sprinkling of sugar dots.

"You promised you'd come."

She turned to Robert's screams. He pressed his back against the sliding glass door, away from Greta. She brought her hands to her face and kneaded sagging wrinkles like soft dough. Swallowing, she tried to smooth her skin and reassure her son with a smile. But her lips grimaced as she bared aching teeth.

"Mamma, please!"

Beneath his wails another sound jolted Greta. A whimper so low she almost didn't hear it. She turned.

There. In the oven. Angela was trussed up on a baking dish like a Christmas turkey, her toes already crisping against the hot sides of the oven and her fine blonde hair giving off the smell of charcoal as it twisted on itself and turned black. Her whimpering continued as her eyes fluttered open and shut and her breath grew ragged.

Baby! The word didn't make it past her stuck throat. She lunged at the oven, meaning to rescue her daughter from its confines, but her hands refused to grip the handle. Angela cried harder.

"Mamma, stop it!"

But Greta couldn't help it. Her hand moved to turn up the oven.

125

With every ounce of new strength the treatment had given her, she forced her hand two knobs over, to the burner with the broken pilot light.

She moaned, a wretched sound, and twisted the knob. A clicking and gentle hiss mixed with the crying and screaming.

"Robert." Her mouth unstuck itself. A grating noise snuck out from her clenched throat. "Get the matches. For birthday cakes."

Robert shook his head and didn't move.

"Robert. Now!" She roared.

The boy edged to a drawer. As he fumbled, Greta remembered his last birthday, how proud he had been lighting his own candles. How many nervous tries he took in front of his friends. He pulled out a small box of matches.

"Light one."

Robert's shaking hands faltered. But after three tries the match struck. His eyes widened at the flame.

"Toss it to me." Greta's voice was more of a growl.

The boy flicked the flame from his fingers. It went out with a wisp of gray smoke.

"Again!" Greta leaned on the knob harder, fighting the twitching within her to remove her hand.

More fumbling. He bit his lip. A flare.

"Walk to me. Slowly." Greta hissed.

Tears spilled down Robert's cheeks, but his legs moved toward her. Three stiff steps and the match caught the cloud of gas. The boy dropped the match and crouched on the floor. A stream of fire caught the fluffy pink of Greta's robe.

Searing pain rushed over Greta's skin as the fire spread. Her robe shriveled and melted against her body. A scream burst from her throat, but to what was left of her ears it sounded more like a cackle as smoke filled her lungs. The sound of a witch.

Robert huddled in the far corner, clutching himself. Greta reached to him. Called to him. The tightness of her skin came apart in wrinkles and she took one fiery step before she fell. Her melting eyes clung to her unmoving child until they saw nothing.

***

Emergency services took Angela from the oven, badly burned but alive, and sealed off the scorched home. Greta's body went to the coroner's office, crisped so black it didn't matter if she was twenty or a hundred. The coroner called Dr. Macy early in the morning.

"I appreciate you letting me look at the brain," Dr. Macy said. "It's a strange side effect."

"I'd say being set on fire is more than a side effect," the coroner snorted. "But your connections reach higher than mine, so have at it."

Dr. Macy bisected the brain with deft hands and, after a cursory inspection, cut thin slices to examine under the microscope. "I just don't understand. Most patients don't even get to the ginger stage."

"The ginger stage?"

"Baking. We can't figure out why it's always ginger. Maybe some kind of immune response triggering a craving in certain women."

The coroner glanced at the report. "Oh, yeah. A gingerbread house was in the kitchen. But they say the boy started the fire."

"She completed three days of neural transfer with him. The boy's brain probably picked up some nanites, and they drove him to light the fire. I just wish I knew why the transfer doesn't work in some pairs. It should be seamless. A younger mother, a calmer kid. Ninety-nine percent of the time it works." He looked away from Greta's brain, considering. "Shit. The nightmares. If he was awake, that would mess with the flow, make the nanites go off-program."

The coroner raised his thin eyebrows. "If the boy has nanites…"

"He'll be fine. Might need therapy as an adult. Lighting your mother on fire can mess with the brain." Dr. Macy pushed the tray with the brain away and removed his gloves. "But that's just one more patient for RejuveNation."

Grady's Dumplings

Dale Hankins

I shot Daddy before I ate his cat. Me and Daddy was in the kitchen. The bulb hanging from the cord in the ceiling swung back and forth shining light and then dark on Daddy's face. The shot from Granddaddy's shotgun took off the top of his head. Brains, blood, and skull flew all over Mamma's rose curtains, the ones she embroidered last spring before the cancer took her. I begged her to stop smoking, but she wouldn't listen. Now there was a bloody mess all over the last pretty thing she made.

Daddy fell and began flopping around – making a real mess. I held him down with the gun barrel while I put a slug in his chest. Maybe it hit his heart. Maybe not. But he stopped flopping.

My hands got bloody as I wiped down the kitchen real good. Mamma always taught us to clean up our own mess. Then I drug Daddy outside and wrapped him in the old tarp we used to cover the tractor with in winter. I went looking for Grady, Daddy's big orange tabby. He hurt my only best friend, Cindy. If Grady had clawed Cindy once he had clawed her a thousand times. Daddy just laughed when Grady did it. Sometimes he pulled Grady's tail to make him even meaner. Them days was over now.

I found Grady crouched down behind the washtub next to the barn. He didn't mew or nothing when I picked him up. He just hung there - a big fat cushion with his legs dangling loose. I carried him to the back porch. His ears went back, and he yowled just before I whacked him with a piece of firewood. I sat on a step and skinned him while I watched the sun come up – dark blue, purple, pink then golden. Cindy always said there wasn't nothing prettier on God's green earth than sunrise. Sometimes she would stare at it so long I worried it would blind her.

I cut Grady up like a squirrel – hindquarters, front legs, neck, and ribs. I stacked the meat in a dishpan and rinsed it off with the garden hose. I put the head, skin, and guts in a pail out by the garage. Mrs. Ashcroft's dogs would have a treat.

Grady barely fit in Mamma's Wearever pot. I filled it with water and turned the heat on low. Grady was tough, but an hour or two in the pot would soften him up just fine.

While Grady cooked, I mixed up some dough for dumplings. When I had a good-sized ball, I floured the cutting board, rolled out the dough and cut it into little squares. I hummed the *Tennessee Waltz* while I worked. Mamma would always smile and twirl whenever she heard that song. I left the dumplings to dry while I washed and cut up the greens.

I put the greens in the Dutch oven. For seasoning, I cut up an onion and some salt pork and put it in the pot. Some vinegar and a dash of sugar would make the greens taste just right.

I froze. What was I doing? Was I crazy or what?

Two of Mamma's main rules was to save salt pork for when all you had was beans and to never, never, ever use her Dutch oven for greens. Too late now. Salt pork was in the greens, they were in the Dutch oven, and Grady was in the Wearever. A real mess. I was glad Mamma wasn't here to see it.

I went back outside and drug Daddy out to the dogwood at the back of the lot. I dug as far down as I could manage and then rolled him in. The dogwood was a good place for Daddy. He would smile every spring when the dogwood bloomed. He'd sit on the back porch smoking a Pall Mall and stare at the flowers. I'd sit watching. Waiting.

Finally, after ever so long, it would come - the tiniest little wrinkle at each corner of his mouth. Then he'd look down at me and his face would turn to stone. That was my signal. I'd run and get the whiskey and he'd pour a little in his coffee. After a while, he would smile again. This time his store-bought teeth would shine, and his eyes would crinkle. Sometimes, he'd reach out and run his hand over my head.

"You sure are a looker, Danny. Yes sir, a real looker."

Mamma would call us in to breakfast. She made the best biscuits you ever tasted, Mamma did. They were just like on television. Steam really did come out when you busted 'em open. The insides was soft and fluffy, perfect for sopping up eggs, red-eye gravy, and cane syrup. Daddy only ever ate the crust. He always pulled the insides out and left them on the side of his plate. Watching his strong fingers crumble up the biscuit and drop it in the juice from his eggs always gave me a funny feeling in my stomach. His Adam's apple would bob up and down as he swallowed. He would lick bits of egg from his fingers and smack his lips.

After breakfast, Daddy would go on out to the shed to sharpen tools or clean his guns. Me and Mamma would go to the garden. Sometimes Cindy would come over to help.

Weeds seemed to come up overnight. We had to keep at them if we wanted to eat. We lived mostly on the garden along with the deer, rabbits, and squirrel that Daddy and me killed. Sometimes Mamma would get us a piece of pork or beef from Piggly Wiggly. But mostly we did just fine with what we could raise or catch. We never went hungry. They was always beans and cornbread.

Most days, after he spent a little time in the shed, Daddy would go on down to the domino hall. Least ways that was where he always said he was going. One time I followed him to see. He caught me at it and gave me the belt so hard it left welts on my legs and back. I never followed him again.

He mostly came home around dark. Sometimes he didn't come back 'til morning, sometimes not for two or three days. Those were the bad times.

Mamma would start in as soon as Daddy opened the door, "Eustus Tucker – you son of a bitch. Where the hell have you been? You expect me to just sit here like a bump on a log while you go off gallivanting around?"

Daddy would pour himself a whiskey, carry the bottle over to the kitchen table, and sit down.

The longer Mamma shouted the louder she got.

"You think I'm your slave or something? You got a woman in town or what? You know my family would have killed you if I hadn't of stopped them. My folks never wanted me to marry white-trash like you!"

For a while Daddy would stare at the tabletop and swig his whiskey like it was water. Once the bottle was almost gone, he'd raise his fist and slam the table so hard it bounced the salt and pepper shakers. He'd whisper in a midnight voice, "You better hush woman."

Mamma never did though. She'd just keep on and on while Daddy's face got redder and redder. Finally, he'd slap her, and she'd throw something at him.

Cindy stayed with us a lot of nights to get away from her Daddy. When things got too bad, we would run and hide under my bed, hugging each other as the thud of his fists carried down the hallway. Mamma would keep shouting for a bit, but soon there wouldn't be nothing but more thumping and then the crying. If the crying went on too long, we'd hear the sound of Daddy's belt whistling through the air to beat her. Her cries was so loud and painful I'd look down to see if my skin wasn't busted open. Cindy and me would just stare into the dark. Not sad. Not afraid. Not nothing. We'd hug each other tighter and tighter while we prayed to the baby Jesus. After a thousand years, Daddy would pull Mamma down the hall to their bedroom. Sometimes when I peeped out the door, I saw him dragging her by her hair.

"No Eustus. Please no! I'm sorry honey. Please no Eustus!"

For a spell, banging and crying would come from their room and then just quiet, like a night with no moon in it. Cindy would sneak on down to the spare bedroom. I'd climb into my bed and lie on my stomach. I never waited long. I'd smell whiskey before the whisper came.

"You awake?"

Never said nothing, just pulled down the covers and pushed my bottom up.

"That's right. That's right sugar. You know what Daddy needs. You're the only who does. The only one who really loves me."

He'd pull down my underpants and rub my butt. The calluses on his hands scratched and made my skin tingle. I'd go

133

someplace else right about then, maybe to the time me and Cindy found that big ol' piece of quartz down by Miller's creek. I could see it sparkle in the sun so clear, bright, and beautiful that I hardly felt it when Daddy shoved into me. Sometimes he used lard but sometimes, like tonight, all he had was spit. It never took long, kinda' like the way I saw horses doing it over at Sadie Jenkins – in and out a few times, lickedy split and that would be all she wrote. I was used to it. I knew he needed it, and besides, if he didn't get it from me, I worried he might get at Cindy. Truth be told, sometimes I rubbed my pecker and squirted while he did it. I never told nobody but Cindy 'bout that. She just giggled.

That was pretty much our days and nights. Time is as time was, like they say. Things changed last spring though. Mamma had always prayed for our deliverance. Didn't seem like Jesus knew our address. He must'a found us last spring cause he took Momma home. Least I hope so.

After Mamma passed, Daddy came at me every night. But he kept away from Cindy - least 'til last night. Last night I wasn't enough. When he was done with me, he went after Cindy. I snuck behind him when he went down to her room. I peeked inside and watched him yank her up from the bed. She screamed.

He was too drunk to notice and too mean to care. He pushed her to her knees and shoved his pecker in her face. She shook her head and turned away. He held the back of her head with one hand and pinched her nose closed until she opened her mouth to breathe. He pushed his pecker in and just held it there. She gagged and beat on his legs. Then he picked her up, threw her down, and pushed into her. His face had a look that would have scared the devil. Spit came from one corner of his mouth. I run over to push him away from Cindy. Saw his fist rise up what seemed a hundred miles, then nothing but white.

When I woke, I was tied to my bed. Daddy stood in the doorway, Light from the hall shined around him, throwing his shadow across my bed.

Some animal I never heard before screamed. "Untie me you bastard! Let me up from here, or I'll kill you! I swear to God I will!"

Daddy growled. "You ain't strong enough to kill a piss ant. You ain't nothin' but your Mamma's little ol' baby girl. Weak as water that's you. All you ever will be."

Couldn't see his eyes but I felt them – burning into me from the doorway. He turned and shuffled down the hallway. I tried to get loose, but he had tied me up good. I pulled and tugged all night bloodying my wrists. Finally, just before daybreak, I got loose.

I crept real careful down to Cindy's room and poked my head inside. "Cindy?"

She didn't say nothing. I moved to the side of her bed and touched her - stone cold. Her blankets were bloody. I kissed her, closed her eyes, and pulled up the covers. I wanted to cry, but a deep hole inside me sucked up all my tears. I lay down next to her and stared up at the ceiling, like we used to do. We'd pretend the stains on the ceiling were butterfly wings, fairy tale people, or maybe maps of some faraway place – a place where me and her would run off to someday. But those was just dreams; right now, I had things to do.

I eased out of bed and down the hall to the gun case. When I got there, I opened the glass door and got the 10-gauge that Grandaddy Tucker had got from his daddy, who got it from his daddy, on back to a time before anybody could remember.

Light shined on the barrel from the kitchen doorway down at the end of the hall. The barrel glowed light blue, like it was shining through water and wasn't quite ready to be real. Dark patterns lined the steel from where it had been folded and beaten back on itself maybe a thousand times. I snapped open the barrel and dropped in two slugs. Slugs don't spread as wide as buck shot but they're better if you want to knock something downright quick. I cocked the hammers and put the stock tight against my shoulder. If you don't hold a big gun tight, it can hurt you. The gun had broke the arms of Tuckers before. I wondered if it had ever killed one.

I walked to the kitchen. Daddy had his back to me pouring another whiskey. When I stepped across the doorway he turned. His head bumped the light bulb hanging from the ceiling. Light and dark chased each other across his face. His eyes were bloody.

He smiled with thin lips and sat the whiskey bottle down real slow. He never took his eyes off me.

"What're you doing?"

"I'm gonna' kill you."

He snorted. "Is that right? What makes you think you can kill me?"

"Cindy," was all I could say.

Daddy closed his eyes. "I never, I never meant to do that son. It was the drink. You know how crazy it makes me."

The gun felt heavy. Daddy opened his eyes and watched the barrel weave. He grinned at me and that was enough. I let loose. Like I said, the first shot took off the top of his head. He would never think up ways to hurt Cindy or me again. The last shot blew open his heart. I would never have to feel it beat against my back in the night. Never, ever again.

After I took care of Daddy and Grady, I sat at the kitchen table and took a deep breath of the dumplings and greens. Mamma and me used to sit at the table in the early morning before getting at the chores. Mamma would bring me "cossie" my pretend coffee, mostly cream and sugar with just enough coffee to turn it brown. We'd would sit and talk real quiet, so as not to wake Cindy and Daddy. It was our special time: the time when she would tell me about when she was a little girl over in Star City putting peanuts in her RC Cola; how her family helped take this land from the Indians; how some of them married Indians; and how she grew up to be a big, tall woman who played basketball like nobody's business. I loved the smell of her cigarettes and how she flicked the ashes into the big green ashtray in the middle of the table. No ashes landed on the table – nary a one. Now the ashtray was empty, and Mamma's smell was so faint I could hardly tell she had ever been here.

I didn't have no cigarettes, so I got up and made cossie. I switched to real coffee last year cause Daddy said it would put hair on my chest. But my chest was still bare, and wasn't nobody around, so I guessed a little cossie wouldn't hurt.

Yessir, cossie would do just fine.

An Odd Gathering of Peculiar Cats

J.D. Harlock

"Revolution may be unbecoming of a true gentlecat, but when shackled with the bonds of servitude of MAN, I say it would be most unbecoming not to revolt!"

-The Catifesto

In an unsuspecting town in the middle of nowhere, cats of all shapes and sizes huddle around Old Whiskers to listen in on what he has to say about the state of cat-dom in the modern world. They have traveled far and wide to hear this speech of his but are disappointed to see that he is not the same cat they had heard so many gush about.

For one, they were told that Mr. Whiskers had fur that reminded one of a mighty lion's mane and piercing blue eyes that looked directly into your soul. But the truth couldn't have been any further from that. Still, they were weary and anxious, and the trip back home was, no doubt, going to be a long one...

***

Having been hoisted onto his platform by a rowdy bunch of local rapscallions with nothing better to do, Old Whiskers stood high above the lowly cats on the back of a rubbish bin with a pleased look on his face, ready to make his grand speech to the unsuspecting cat public. Though they were not one to judge a cat by the way he or she dressed, many of the older members of the audience couldn't help but notice that Old Whiskers was quite fashionably costumed (considering the circumstances) in high waisted silk pants held up by silk suspenders with a loose white silk shirt and a silk suit with a matching silk vest. On this one cat (granted this rather large cat) was more silk than they'd ever seen in their entire lives here in this alley, and probably ever would, once he departed to what they were told was pressing work elsewhere. Never ones for envy, they were still not too sure how they felt about the matter and didn't quite know what to make of it, but, as was the case with all that troubled the prolecatiat, not one soul said a thing about the matter that irked them so. They knew it to be impertinent and unbecoming of true gentlecats and gentlekits.

***

Before he was to begin, Old Whiskers pounded on his chest to clear a throat clogged up with some rather unsavory hairballs that would have been best dealt with in private. The cats in the audience watched him with an awkward patience usually reserved for that one acquaintance who pleasured himself rather eagerly in public without having the decency to ask others to join in.

"Fellow felines!" Old Whiskers suddenly called out with gusto once he got that last pesky hairball out that had been inconveniencing him since last night's debauch, "I say Fellow felines, lend me your ears!"

Normally, there would be some mumbling and grumbling

here and there, but this time, this one time, the cats all suddenly went quiet— every single one. Not a meow could be heard in that alley, and not a breath could be felt.

And that was the way Old Whiskers liked it.

He was quite aware that the cats had been caught off guard by his magnificent voice (that from an early age had been trained in the art of sesquipedalian loquaciousness) and utterly relished in it.

But that was not hard to see.

For if one looked closely, they would have seen a slight toothy smile at the tip of Old Whiskers's mouth that he couldn't help himself with.

"Ha!" He thought to himself, "I have them now..."

Because that was usually all it took.

Old Whiskers then cleared his throat again, licked his mouth, and dove into his speech as a panther would his prey. "My fellow felines! I humbly commend you for taking the time and effort to join me today on this most wondrous occasion. For you see, the days where we subject ourselves to the whims and fancies of man are over!"

Old Whiskers took a deep breath in anticipation of his audience's applause, but the cats in the audience were not entirely sure what he meant. In hushed tones, they hissed to one another questions whose answers they could not even fathom, for their gentle souls would not allow it.

But before they could speculate as to what in bloody hell he was talking about, Old Whiskers raised his paw to the sky...

"The time has come for us to take our fates into our own hands and unshackle ourselves from our bonds of servitude."

And the cats in the audience suddenly froze in their places as if they'd just spotted a hound near the alley, for they could not even begin to parse through what they had just stood witness to. They had been made aware of the talk surrounding Old Whiskers' eccentricities by visitors but would never have imagined that a cat of his caliber would call for the ultimate act of treachery!

"Blasphemy!" Someone cried out. It was Little Tugger, a young orange cat who was just beginning to understand how disappointing the adult world would be.

"Who was that?!" Old Whiskers looked around.

The cats turned their attention to Little Tugger, who had gotten out of his rather uncomfortable seat in protest. They'd never thought much of him before (mainly because he never seemed to think much of them), but they needed some form of guidance, and Little Tugger would have to do.

"Blasphemy!" He cried out again, "The humans have been nothing but good to us. They have fed us when we starved and fondled us when we froze! They have shown us a kindness we can never repay! Shame on you! Shame on you, I say!"

Many of the older cats in the audience nodded in agreement and muttered their affirmations. However, the younger cats were not entirely sure where they stood on this matter and felt strangely detached from the young cat who looked like them and talked like them and was around their age, but who did not fit in and probably never would.

"Maybe cats were in need of a change?" They found themselves thinking.

"Now, kit—" Old Whiskers tried to reason with his young adversary, "We must not waste this golden opportunity!"

He could feel that he was losing his audience. Perhaps it was not the right time to begin targeting alleys of a "lower" disposition.

"Shame!" Little Tugger raised his paw, "Shame!"

Old Whiskers could not have loathed this little kit more. If only he could get him alone and have his henchcats rub his tummy vigorously. But for now, a change of pace would do. A change of pace would do.

"Can you not see it, my furry little friend?" Old Whiskers said to Little Tugger, even though he was not addressing him at all, "Can you not see the glorious future that awaits us in ecatcipation?"

The younger cats in the audience nodded in agreement. Realizing that he couldn't possibly get through to him, Old Whiskers would instead try to appeal to the masses. But Little Tugger had had enough. He had been talked down to his entire life by those who thought they were wiser when they weren't and those who thought they knew when they didn't.

No more!

Now was the time to speak!

Now was the time to act!

Now was the hour of his triumph!

He curled his tiny paw into a fist and raised it to the air!

"I see empty bowls!" He cried out with the fiery passion of a thousand wet cats, "And dirty litter boxes that will never be clean again."

"Now, now, young cat. We cannot let ourselves be subjugated by our own indolence." Old Whiskers brought his arms to his puffed-up chest and pulled on his suspenders.

Old Whiskers turned to address good old Fluffer Nutter, an affable chap who was as reliable as he was dense.

"Fluffer Nutter, were you not asked to exit your own house to relieve yourself in the streets like some low-bred rapscallion?"

"It's true, I was, boss…"

"Aha!"

"Wait... how did he know that..."

Old Whiskers then turned to Mrs. Furball, a house cat who was as agreeable as she was aloof.

"And Mrs. Furball, wasn't Mr. Furball's masculinity so cruelly stripped from him when he was but a young tomcat?"

"Yes, he spends his day now playing with balls of yarn and huffing catnip."

"Aha!" Old Whiskers then turned to indomitable Mr. Wiggles, "And you, Mr. Wiggles!"

"Yes?"

Old Whiskers was really relishing the moment now, for he had a real showstopper in store for Mr. Wiggles! But before he could ask, Old Whiskers suddenly found himself exclaiming:

"Ah! They're here! They're finally here!"

For the catvalry had arrived.

A group of peculiar cats gathered around under Old Whiskers' garbage can to sit in the two rows of fine pawchairs reserved for them.

"Allow me, everyone, to introduce to you fine gentlecats and gentlekits, the Central Committee!"

"Of what?!" Little Tugger cried out.

"Of the Brotherhood, of course."

Little Tugger then noticed a banner being propped up above their heads, and on it was written in bold gold "The Revolutionary Brotherhood of Friendly Friends."

"They seem friendly. " Mrs. Furball said earnestly even though to Little Tugger the central committee seemed to be primarily composed of stodgy, old creatures who dressed in a catter not too dissimilar to Old Whiskers's and probably thought of themselves in a catter not too dissimilar to Old

Whiskers either.

"If you don't mind my asking, boss. But why are they here?" Fluffer Nutter asked, confused (as he tended to be), "And how did you know that about the—"

"—why, my good cat? Well, these gentlecats are the greatest minds of their generation," Old Whiskers waved his arms theatrically, "and together, we've written a catifesto!"

"A catifesto, boss?"

"Yes, a most wondrous catifesto!" Old Whiskers exclaimed, looking quite satisfied with himself.

"And what about the other question?"

"One that will steer the fate of catkind into the future!"

"What's in it, boss?" Fluffer Nutter asked earnestly, "and why do you keep ignoring my other question?"

"That's of little concern now…." Old Whiskers waved his paw dismissively, "What matters is that we've all agreed to adhere to it."

"Can we take a look at this document?" Little Tugger asked, losing patience with the whole charade.

"I'm afraid," Old Whiskers tugged at his collars, "that it's still under revision pending approval of the board, the shadow committee, the politburo, and the—" Old Whiskers trailed off absentmindedly as he tried to come up with a more satisfactory answer, "Etcetera, etcetera, I'm sure a consummate witling like yourself is aware of how these things go…"

"Enough of this nonsense!" Little Tugger snapped, "Why are we here?!"

"Simple, my kit!" Old Whiskers bellowed, "The committee and I have fought long and hard to secure the means by which we could unshackle ourselves from that foul blight."

It was as if Old Whiskers truly believed the nonsense he had just uttered. All he needed now was the confirmation of an audience slavishly devoted to him, and the members of the central committee were more than happy to oblige.

"Orthodox!" One mumbled to himself.

"Most orthodox!" Another mumbled.

"Yes, most orthodox indeed!" A third joined in.

And that was as much excitement as the central committee could muster. Not that they wanted to muster any more than that or that they needed to. Old Whiskers' rather lively showcatship had more than compensated for their orderliness in the past, and there was no reason for it to fail them now.

"And by Bastet! I think we've finally got it!" Old Whiskers proclaimed as a contraption was wheeled in below him. It was hidden under a fine silk cover that few of the cats seemed to realize was worth more than all the wealth they had accumulated in their lives combined. Not that it mattered, of course. Because after that cover was removed, their lives would never be the same...

***

A white cat dressed in a lab coat and goggles somehow emerged from a shadowy corner of the alley that they'd never really noticed before to remove those white silk covers. Although they were not ones to pay any heed to a cat's appearance, the cats of the alley couldn't help but notice that on his strange face was the most frightening smile they had ever seen.

"Now, my felines!" Old Whiskers stretched his arms far and wide as if he saw the entire world held between his two paws, "Witness the dawn of the Cat!"

The cats in the audience suddenly froze in fear. They had little idea of what to make of any of this and even less when the blanket was removed, for they found themselves gawking at a pointed contraption of steel and steam, unlike anything the world had seen before.

"What is it?" Fluffer Nutter asked as the white cat eagerly hopped into the seat to operate it.

"A LASER!" Old Whiskers exclaimed, then began to laugh maniacally.

"What's that?"

"Uhm… erm…" Old Whiskers pulled at his collar.

"Oh, can we see it in action?" Mrs. Furball asked.

"Uhm, yes, why not… we're due for a demonstration at some point or another." Old Whiskers mumbled, then turned to the white cat, who ushered to his filthy assistants with his paws. The filthy assistants adjusted the odd contraption, directing it at the brick alley wall.

"Any volunteers?" Old Whiskers asked, studying the audience in the process, but no cat was brave enough to come forward. That is, no cat but a little kit who was eagerly hopping up and down on his chair with his paw in the air.

That kit, dear reader, was Tiny Tim, an orphan whose cheerful disposition hid the pain brought on by a life of hardship on the cold, harsh streets of cat-dom. But in spite of it all, Tim, dear Tim, had the biggest of hearts and purest of intentions, so much so that the cat community had decided unanimously to take him in as one of their own. Everyone loved Tiny Tim, and Tiny Tim loved all.

"May I?" He asked with that little gleam in his eye.

"Uhmm…" Old Whiskers pulled at his collar, managing to rip a bit of the fabric, "why not? Sure, my kit…."

Tiny Tim promptly left his seat and was escorted to the wall.

"You'd all be better off if you follow in Tiny Tim's example…

" Old Whiskers muttered hurriedly, then turned to the white cat. "Now then, is everything in place?"

The white cat gave him a paws up.

"Excellent... Uhm... Just to be clear. This hasn't been tested yet... Uhm... I must inform you all of something... I'm afraid this is..."

But before he could finish, the lever was very eagerly pulled by the white cat, and the contraption began to rumble, slowly building up momentum until beams of light shot out from all over its dish and met at the pointer. The machine began to shake violently as a furious ball of crimson began forming in it. It seemed as if something was about to erupt, and the cats in the audience, both young and old, rose in anticipation and anxiousness.

"What's going on?" Mrs. Furball asked.

"Papa, I'm scared." An innocent kit told his bewildered father.

Tiny Tim stood there on the wall, wide-eyed, his chimney sweeper cap in his hands. He had never known true fear before that moment, and it was now making an awfully unpleasant introduction. Thinking it was only a moment before he met his doom at the hands of this mad contraption, Tiny Tim closed his eyes and prayed to Bastet for mercy.

As a tear rolled down his furry little cheek, the laser finally fired a violent beam, unlike anything the world had seen before, straight at the poor, gentle soul filled with regret that could not have possibly known what he had volunteered for. But it was all right, for Tiny Tim had made his peace with his past and was ready to move on to the next life—

Except, he was still in the alley!

He stood by the wall, shivering, as his little paws shook his little flat cap and his eyelids squirmed as he struggled to keep them closed. Surely, he must be dead and in the Great Litter Box in the sky?

Tiny Tim slowly opened up one of his eyes to take a peek at the new home for his immortal soul but shut them again when he heard the most obnoxious sound...

"Ha!" Little Tugger exclaimed, "Nothing happened!"

Old Whiskers, on the other hand, pulled on his suspenders, in triumph for he was rather proud of himself.

"On the contrary, my dear kit," Old Whiskers ushered to Tiny Tim with a smile, "Look!"

On closer inspection, Little Tugger noticed a rather odd mark on the little kit's face. A dot, if you will. A crimson red one right above his cute little eyes. Tiny Tim's pupils moved upwards to try and take a look at it.

"What's going on?" Little Tugger asked.

But Tiny Tim was too distracted by the dot to answer.

Because...

He. just. couldn't. seem. to. grab. it....

And when it moved, Tiny Tim felt. compelled. to. follow. it.

But then it moved again.

And so did he.

And again.

And so did he.

And again.

And again.

And again.

He suddenly found himself on his knees like some rapscallion trying to catch it.

"Is this it?" Little Tugger asked, trying to suppress his laughter.

But then the cats suddenly all rose up around him!

"Where are you all going?!" Little Tugger asked in disbelief. "You can't possibly be fooled by this..."

Though they just barely managed to register what he was saying, the cats in the audience were well enough aware to continue disregarding anything Little Tugger had to say about anything as they always had and would. For the life of them, they could not tell what compelled them to. But compelled they were...

They all huddled around the dot, trying to pounce on it, but. they. just. couldn't. seem. to. grab. it...

As their frustrations inevitably got out of hand, few of them could even get close to the damned thing without putting up a fight.

Early on, Mrs. Furball asserted her dominance over the pack as she viciously fought anyone who got near it with her chiseled, manicured nails. However, try as she might, she. just. couldn't. grab. it.

The cats slowly lost their minds, each failure driving them into a greater frenzy than the last. Their exasperation was evident, and their rage was palpable. In her madness, Mrs. Furball grabbed a fishbone off the ground and raised it to the heavens as she let out her primal scream...

Anarchy was set loose upon the alley that day as the cats' baser instincts utterly decimated the last ounces of their civility.

"This is what I was afraid of," Old Whiskers sighed as he dabbed his head with a piece of silk.

He then waved his arms high above his head, trying to usher to the strange white cat, who seemed to be enjoying the scene quite a bit. A tad too much, perhaps...

"Shut it off!" Old Whiskers called out, "Shut the blasted thing off, doctor!"

His smile visibly turning to a frown, the white cat dutifully complied, and that was the end of his fun.

***

The cats slowly awoke from their feverish nightmare, unsure of what had just taken place. They found themselves in the process of some savage act they were utterly shocked to have partaken in. But, more importantly, their fur was a mess, and their clothes were all tattered and torn.

"Now then," Old Whiskers was still dabbing his forehead with a cloth, "Where were we—"

"—You monster!" Little Tugger cried out in anger and disgust as he slowly emerged from the rubbish bin he'd taken refuge in. "What were you planning to do with this… this… abomination?"

"Why, it's simple, my kit, with this marvelous contraption, I will throw the human world into disarray. All it will take is for us to introduce it town to town, city to city, and country to country, in turn demonstrating our power over them. Though there may be those who doubt our genteel modus operandi, the humans will have no choice but to bow down to the might of our machine and thus in our own munificence begins the AGE OF CAT!"

"By Bastet…." Little Tugger muttered in disbelief.

"Oh, I'm sure you're very concerned about your human compatriots Little Tugger, but rest assured my kit. There is a place for you among us." Old Whiskers straightened his back all the way upright. "Your lack of catters and complete disregard for the admiration of your peers has impressed me tonight, and I'm sure that the Central Committee would agree."

"Orthodox—"

150

"Not now!" Old Whiskers lashed out before yowling at them and stomping his legs— then he promptly turned back to Little Tugger. "And because we are an eleemosynary organization, I have decided to make you an offer…"

"I—" Little Tugger interrupted.

"If you behave yourself, I'm prepared to offer you a position in our organization."

"And what would this position be, might I ask?" Little Tugger tapped his paw impatiently.

"You, Little Tugger, will be appointed the leader of the opposition in our fledgling enterprise."

"…"

"All we ask is that you be catting, be catterly, and cattificent."

"…"

"But this must not interfere with your loyalty to the opposition, of course."

"…"

"And I must say, it would do you rather well to bathe now and again." Old Whiskers huffed in high dudgeon, "The other cats in the audience just look uncomfortable. I mean, if you've ever wondered why kittens won't frolic with you, Little Tugger—"

Little Tugger breathed in and out very slowly as he gripped and released his paw in tandem.

"Little Tugger?"

He walked to the center of the alley.

"Little Tugger, what are you going to do?" Old Whiskers's dichroic eyes closely followed Tugger as he traipsed towards his destiny.

"My fellow felines," Little Tugger did not address Old Whiskers nor speak to him, "One day when cat supremacy has twisted and contorted us so that cat-dom more resembles the human world than it does the feline one, we will look back on this day and wonder how we could have strayed so far out of owners' homes and left the flap open so pugnaciously. On this day, we would know that we chose to abandon our ways to follow *him,* knowing what we were going to do and who we were going all because some flagitious ne'er-do-well came to us in silk, no less, promising us catifestos and committee masquerading as ecatcipation. And I say to you my fellow felines that if the Dawn of the Cat is brought about by an ecatcipation through our blind and willing submission to charlatans, then the dusk will soon follow and no cat may meow on that day!"

And the cats in the alley were silent. All of them but one.

"Do you understand what we are about to do cat?" Old Whiskers cried out in frustration, "Do you understand?! If this is what one can do to a gathering of alley cats, imagine what hundreds, maybe even thousands, can do to mankind itself!" Old Whisker raised his jittery paw to the sky. "Order! Civility! Proper attire! All will be lost to anarchy at the flash of a laser!"

"Arrogance! Foolishness! Madness!" Tugger wailed against the sheer audacity of the fat cat that dared to speak such sin, "You think man has the capacity to not adhere to proper dress code!"

"Listen, you mumpismus smellfungus," Old Whiskers' shook his tiny paw in unbridled rage, "My final offer is this: if you cease your senseless senselessness, I am prepared to—"

"Yes." Little Tugger tapped his paws impatiently again.

"Allow you in practicable consignments—"

"Yes."

"Your very own—"

"Yes."

152

"Cat nip."

"..."

"Of course, this is pending the approval of the board, the shadow committee, the politburo, and the—"

"THAT'S IT!"

Little Tugger roared and Old Whiskers was taken aback in fright.

"Now, Little Tugger, you must calm down!" Old Whiskers tried to ease the tension for once. "This is unbecoming of a true gentle cat—"

"How dare you... How dare you think in your rambunctious catnip fancies that I would ever even consider desecrating myself with such filth?"

"But it'll allow you to be less—"

"Less? Less!" Little Tugger's eyes were about to burst, "Less what?"

"Uhm... less difficult...."

"You... You... DOG!" Little Tugger screamed bloody murder, slandering Old Whiskers with the word that no gentlecat dare utter lest they lose their standing in society forever...

However, Old Whiskers wasn't fazed. With the air of a schoolteacher who thought quite highly of himself, he snorted then retorted with a sneer: "We cannot simply halt cat kind's progress so that we may consider something as unimportant as the ethical ramifications of our actions." He grew more anxious as his little act dragged on. "Why, where would we be had we not engineered the Canine-Rodent Tussle of '48 or had we not interfered in the Fowl Civil War of—"

"Enough! The humans must be warned!" Little Tugger had had it. "This madness must be put to an end!"

But Old Whiskers had had it too, and unlike Little Tugger,

had the resources to deal with his nuisance.

"Seize him!" He shouted from the top of his lungs, ruffling his pristine fur in the process.

And naturally, the members of the central committee reacted in kind.

"Orthodox!" One proclaimed.

"Most orthodox!" Another proclaimed.

"Most orthodox, indeed!" A third joined in.

A group of cats shrouded in black garbs suddenly gathered behind Little Tugger. He had not seen them up to this point and could not even hear them as they approached him. One of them, their leader perhaps, put his paw on Little Tugger's shoulder.

"Now, Little Tugger, we will do you no harm," Old Whiskered chuckled as he twirled his magnificent whiskers, "You'll just be sent to a lovely camp where we can iron out these 'idiosyncrasies' of yours."

Little Tugger's eyes grew wide with fear. This was it. This was really it. He knew he was not long for this world. But, somehow, he always knew that. He... He always knew—

"—Oi!" Someone suddenly called out with his rather coarse voice. Without the need to make sure, Old Whiskers's head sunk into his shoulders in disturbance and shame. This was the first time in his life that he had been caught off guard like this. The first time...

And there was nothing that he could do about it.

So all the cats in the alley slowly turned around to face the speaker with the most innocent looks and the most innocent eyes they could muster up (except for Little Tugger, of course, who had the most obnoxious smile on his furry little face).

But the man called out again in a tone more abrasive than

the last:

"Ha! Come and take a look at this!"

"What is it?" His friend replied.

"It's funny," He cackled, "There's an odd gatherin' of some awfully peculiar cats...."

Magnetization and Resistance

Arasibo Campeche

"No caigo en ese truco dos veces. Ese perro ya me mordió."
"I'm not falling for that trick twice. That dog already bit me."

-Puerto Rican saying

The elevator stopped on the second floor of the university's chemistry building, and Bárbara poked her head out to make sure the hallway was empty. The smell of antiseptic came from the labs, but there was no one around.

She hurried past the third lab to her right, where she'd conducted organic chemistry research for the last 30 years, steeling herself to avoid of thinking of the golden days of her work, before being fired. Instead, she filled the compartment where grief goes with hate for the robots.

The second-floor bathroom was also empty. She crouched under the sink, grabbed a vacuum-sealed plastic package hidden behind the plumbing, then slid it into her coat's inside pocket.

She'd been extra careful these past few days while moving wastebaskets with small amounts of used toilet paper from the bathrooms to the lab that had the vacuum sealer. She'd needed to collect nearly every wastebasket in the building since most people flushed their toilet paper. She got back in the elevator, pushed the button marked B, and told herself to not wimp out. If everything went well, her actions wouldn't hurt any real people.

The elevator ride gave her enough time to go over her the last couple of months in her mind. Her stellar record at graduating students, generating innovative scientific ideas and years of work hadn't been enough to keep her researcher job away from the hands of a robot. Last year—thanks to the tenure revocation laws—Bárbara had been re-assigned to custodian duties until she retired, and despite her newly found permanent depression, tried to make the best of it. At least, she hadn't been fired and abandoned like so many other people in similar positions, but that kind of luck didn't strike the same place twice.

Her role in the university had changed, but her passion for teaching remained strong. No one cared if she helped students during her free time. Yet, remembering the meeting she had the week before made Barbara's teeth clench in anger as she made her way through the building's basement.

Derrick Rhodes, the school's dean of Robotic and Automated Labor had given her his personal promise that the new robot would only take half her custodian shift for a short time, and that replacement was out of the question.

"After a couple of weeks, the robot will be evaluated. If it passes the test phase—which they always do—it'll be assigned elsewhere." Rhodes had even attempted to rationalize the situation by saying, "Why not let them do the jobs that they're better at than we are? I'd let them have my job if they had enough of the human touch required to do it."

Somehow Bárbara had doubted he'd give his job away so easily—never mind the fact that it was inane to think that an administrator needed a human touch to do his job—but she had other problems. Not only did a robot steal her previous job, but its scientific output was also outstanding. Objectively, a future when artificial intelligence evolved beyond human understanding was unavoidable. Still, the void left after losing her lab felt like she'd been dismissed from human productivity.

She checked her phone. It was nearly 6 am. The robot custodian's shift had finished almost half an hour before. She made her way to the lab in the basement to find the usual pristine scene the robot left behind. The floor was immaculately clean, chairs and tables polished so carefully they could be thought of as new—the robot's efforts were worthy of envy to anyone who cared. Bárbara cared. She didn't stand a chance. It had even scraped the pieces of chewing gum from under the tables. Hopefully, the gum would find its way into his cogs and give him a mechanical stroke.

She walked around the room, reconsidering her plan. Perhaps sabotaging the robots and having them removed wasn't the strongest approach, but for now it was the only idea she had. She only needed to be employed a few more years before being able to retire, anyway.

A white cylinder, ten feet tall and seven feet wide, occupied the center of the basement. Inside, magnetic slabs surrounded a solenoid micro coil. Orange traffic cones sat on the floor, forming a circular perimeter around the cylinder, indicating how far the magnetic field reached. Red tape ran along the floor, below where the cones should go, in case they were moved by accident. Erased credit cards were the most common victims for students who forgot to empty their pockets before approaching the magnet. This technology had applications ranging from drug discovery to MRI. A few more scientific instruments sat in the chemistry department's basement, but nuclear magnetic resonance spectroscopy, NMR, was Bárbara's expertise, and this NMR instrument was like her baby.

Two of her previous students had complained about issues with the NMR's software, and the thought of fixing it had kept her up the night before. Despite being in a hurry, Bárbara sat in front of the computer linked to the NMR and spent a couple of minutes debugging the system by updating lines of computer code. After finishing, she was certain that the computer would obey her absolutely.

Immediately after, she opened the vacuum sealed package she'd hid in the bathroom and removed some of the contents with a pair of tongs. Used toilet paper hung like poisonous tentacles.

The stench reminded her of a gas station bathroom. With an outstretched arm, she wiped the countertops until the stink became overwhelming, then threw the paper in the wastebasket by the front door. She turned the lights off and fast walked to the parking lot like a saboteur who'd left a ticking bomb behind. No doubt the mess would be cleaned up as soon as it was reported, but hopefully enough PR damage would be done.

In the parking lot, a metallic clanking came from behind her after she opened her car door. She turned to see a robot standing with palms resting over what looked like a third trimester pregnancy belly. The bulbous, distended midsection was designed to store tools. The engineers claimed this way the robot's hands were free from having to carry baggage, efficient. Aesthetically, the designers also claimed that male looking robots with pregnancy bellies made them look more trustworthy.

"Hello, my name is John John," the robot said, then raised one of its hands to wave before letting it fall on its belly with a clunk.

The robot leaned forward, pivoting on its waist, as if its feet were glued to the floor. Plastic, unfocused eyes stared at Bárbara. A pale, waxy material served as the robot's skin. John John wore a blue jumpsuit with a circular hole in the middle to accommodate the robot's midsection; its eyelids clicked with each blink.

The robot read her name tag. "You're Bárbara Morales. What a nice coincidence. I just finished my duties and have been waiting for the bus for 20 minutes, but it's great to meet you. I thought today was your day off. I am the new sentient unit delivered to split the night shift with you. I am sure you have many questions, but don't worry, I am not here to replace you, only to help. I am also well versed in human psychology and can serve as a friend, and we can discuss any frustrations you have." John John straightened, waited, then continued babbling. "I am also shy. I know transitions are hard, yet I am sure ours will be easier. Dean Rhodes informed me you were from Puerto Rico," the robot winked, "I know you have already adapted from life in another country, even another language. Fortunately, you only need enough English to get by. No one judges people by their accents. In fact, I'm not even a person," John John laughed while moving his head from side to side like an inverted pendulum, "making my situation worse than yours."

Bárbara opened her mouth, nearly reciting every swear word she knew in both English and Spanish but thought better of it. An outburst of anger would only arouse suspicion.

"So, what do you say, Bárbara Morales. Can we be colleagues? And keep this place clean and the research and teaching ongoing for many years to come?"

Bárbara exhaled a long breath and unclenched her stomach, smiled, then said, "No hablo Inglés." She got in her car and drove off.

***

She came in half an hour before her shift started on the next afternoon. Only the two undergraduate students she often helped with classes occupied the basement. No emails describing an unexplainable reek of urine had been sent. An administrator somewhere had to be keeping it quiet.

One of the students stood in front of the chemical fume hood. The other sat near the computer, swiping through her phone.

"What sample are you preparing?" Bárbara asked.

Michael, the student working in the fume hood, turned. "Just a quick test sample to make sure the tube is clean." He handled the thin, straw-like NMR tube deftly, preventing any damage to the clear borosilicate glass.

Lisa, still looking at her phone said, "Hi, Dr. Morales."

"Hi."

Bárbara let a few moments pass. "Do you guys know if anything happened here today?"

They shook their heads, seemingly without giving the question a second thought.

Nothing she could do then. "Put your phone away so we can

start." Bárbara waited for Michael to walk over, and until the phones and wallets were in a basket by the table. In addition to credit cards, any electronics could be damaged if too close to the magnet. She entered a command in the computer and told Michael, "Go put the sample in."

"I'm still glad you take out of your time to teach us, Dr. Morales, especially when you don't have to. The robots are like mobile audiobooks. I don't learn anything in class. It's awful," Lisa said.

Robots "taught" by reading textbooks out loud in a non-inflected, accent-free voice, eliminating stylistic differences that led humans to be labeled as good or bad teachers.

Now, all teachers were equal.

Exorbitant increases in tuition rates had allowed the school to swap cheap adjunct professors for objective machines. Many supporters claimed that robot instructors improved teaching to the same extent that a calculator was better than an abacus.

"Let me see what you need to do for class," Bárbara said to Lisa, who passed her a notebook opened near the middle. A slew of differential equations, complex diagrams, and instructions covered the page. Turning the page, Bárbara found more math that she recognized as a formalized theory justifying why NMR worked, how similar it was to an MRI done in a hospital setting, alongside more drawings of nuclei spin systems flipping in and out of Boltzmann distributions.

"I'm guessing this is gibberish to you," Bárbara said.

"The robot is reading the first few chapters of an advanced physics' book in class. But I'm pre-med and haven't taken calculus yet," Michael said.

This is like teaching someone how to read by giving them a dictionary, Bárbara thought.

"My parents are forcing me to stay in school, because they think that as long as I do my best, I'll be okay. They like to emphasize that doctors aren't being replaced," Michael said. "But we all know the truth. Doctors aren't being replaced *yet*."

Bárbara nodded. The rationale behind what jobs were given to robots eluded everyone except the policy makers in charge. Priests and politicians were off-limits since these required "an irrational and loving human heart", yet teachers, service industry workers, and scientists had been deemed obvious choices since their duties were thought to be easily automated. Universal basic income was also being discussed, but unlike passing laws that allowed robots to replace people in their jobs—despite in place protections such as tenure professorship—deciding how much and when to pay the displaced workers was "the trickiest economic problem of our times" and hence no legislation had been passed.

"You're driving the NMR today, Lisa," Bárbara said.

Lisa wrote the commands Bárbara told her and hit go. Instead of one signal for chloroform, the computer screen was sprinkled with thin peaks.

"What's this?" Michael asked.

Lisa shook her head. "Garbage. You contaminated it."

"No. I didn't," Michael said, then shook his head rapidly, as if shedding away the possibility that he made a mistake. "I cleaned everything as best as I could."

Bárbara stood and walked to the fume hood. "Come here for a minute." When both students walked over, she pointed to a warped plastic pipette beside the chloroform bottle. "It's melted."

Michael let out a frustrated sigh. Lisa rolled her eyes.

"I forgot. Plastic dissolves in chloroform," Michael said.

163

"It happens to everybody; don't worry. Find a new bottle and make it again." Bárbara said.

The door opened and she saw her supervisor, Adrián, shyly signal her over.

"Bárbara, can we talk?" he asked, fumbling his fingers in front of his chest. She made the most innocent looking expression she could muster, told the students to continue on their own, and followed Adrián outside.

"Something happened this morning or last night. I don't know," he said.

Here it comes, she thought. "What?" she asked with a straight face.

"Well…"

"Adrián que pasó—"

He put his hand up. "It's better if we stick to English while on campus. Some professors get irritated when we speak Spanish."

Bárbara sighed, forcing several comments addressing Adrián's lack of character to the back of her mind. "Okay."

Adrián pulled her away from the door and spoke in a quiet voice. "This morning, I found toilet paper in that room's trash can."

Bárbara pointed behind her shoulder with her thumb. "Where? In here. I've never seen people cleaning the lab glassware with toilet paper, but maybe it leaves less scratches. Who knows?" She shrugged.

Adrián frowned, and his lips curved downward as if gravity was pulling them off his face. "It was used. And an awful smell everywhere. Luckily, I doused everything in bleach hours before anyone walked in."

Bárbara cupped her hand over her mouth, unable to decide

if her performance was award winning quality or over the top. "That's horrible. It might be the anti-robot protesters. They probably caught on that one has been assigned with us. They do all sorts of vandalism." She paused for a few seconds, wanting to push Adrian's thinking in the right direction without being too obvious. "On the other hand, how does the robot clean? Does it keep all the trash in its belly and move from place to place? Maybe it forgot. You know, they can't smell the same way we do. Sure, they can detect volatiles in the parts per billion range but who knows."

"I'm told the chance that the robot made a mistake is very low. If one of the professors that opposes robot workers finds out, it would start some serious gossip."

"Maybe it's for the best. If they can't do the job, then that's that."

"No, Bárbara. The best is to keep our heads down and follow the rules." His face reddened, but he continued in a whisper. "Did you have anything to do with this? This is one of the robot's first few shifts shared with you. This could look bad on all of us. I'm your supervisor and I wouldn't want to be associated with—"

Barbara raised her hand. She felt betrayed. "I'd appreciate that you don't spread rumors and lies if you don't have any proof. I have a family too and need this job as much as you do. And don't worry, your English is better than mine and you're whiter than me. We won't be lumped together."

"That's not what I meant."

After a moment, Adrián spoke. "Let's keep this between us for now. Rhodes knows of course. He told me he'd take care of it."

"Okay. I need to clock in. Excuse me." Bárbara walked away.

She didn't smile and giggle until she reached the restroom and made sure she was alone. The wastebaskets in the stalls had a few pieces of paper again. After a couple of days of collecting more paper she could repeat her plan. If she made John John look like incompetent nitwit repeatedly, he'd surely get decommissioned. Next time, she'd make sure someone apart from Adrián found her work first.

***

The next day, Bárbara listened to music on her phone while cleaning. Her shift flew by before she knew it as she sang along with one of her favorite Salsa songs, *Todo tiene su final, nada dura para siempre…* All things end, nothing lasts forever.

She stopped singing when John John walked in. Another robot, with the same plastic-white, pasty face followed.

"Hi Bárbara. This is Mike," John John said.

"Mike Mike?" Bárbara asked, smiling.

"No. Just Mike." The other robot said.

"I know. It's a joke."

Both robots looked at each other, then turned back to her, and tilted their heads from left to right while cackling.

"Mike is our new supervisor," John John said after they quieted down.

"What about Adrián?" Barbara's smile disappeared.

"He was let go," Mike said. Both robots lowered their heads as if taking a moment of silence for the recently deceased.

Confusion mixed with anger grabbed at her throat. "What? Why did—"

"Bárbara, I know you're upset. Let me explain." Mike inhaled and sighed, despite having no need for oxygen. "Usually, humans in supervisory positions are not eligible for labor substitution, but it's better for our learning experience if we remain with those who are the same as us. We are more comfortable. We learn from our experiences but also from each other. It's exponentially better this way. Of course, the goal is to approach being more human, which I hope to achieve after supervising you."

Bárbara hid her trembling fists behind her back. She nearly asked if they knew what irony was. Intense pressure pounded on her temples and she squeezed her eyes shut.

"Are you okay? Women of your age are at an increased risk of heart-related incidents. Before coming here, my programmer said that it is better to ignore things one cannot change," Mike said.

"I'm fine," Bárbara said through trembling lips.

Mike nodded and turned to John John, unlatching the lid on top of John John's belly. Screwdrivers and wrenches clinked against metal as he pulled them out.

"Are you guys handy*men* now too?" She yelled.

Both robots laughed.

"We are practicing hand-eye coordination. Every model is different. I'll email you a set of tasks aimed at optimizing your productivity. Especially—" Mike continued talking as Bárbara stormed out of the room.

Bárbara cried as she slammed her fist against her car's steering wheel. The robots would eventually take all the jobs, and she'd done her best to keep her own. Getting Adrián fired in the process wasn't her intention. If only the robots hadn't been slowly taking her job away a second time, none of this would've happened. Sending Mike after John John had "fucked up" was the stupidest approach towards solving the problem, like overlaying two Band-Aids over a deep gushing wound. She wiped her tears with the back of her hand and took a few deep breaths. Guilt gripped her chest like a vise. Adrián's persistence to not speak Spanish in public was only one aspect of his personality she detested. Yet, he didn't deserve to get fired and have his family suffer, much less for actions he didn't commit.

In other industries, such as truck driving and fast-food restaurants, robots had taken over nearly every job, and no number of protests—violent or otherwise—had led to change. A lucky few had received nice pensions or were in situations like Bárbara, but for the most part, people were fired without a second thought.

The next step in labor substitutions had had a larger financial aim. Every news outlet summarized it with the same question: Could robots outthink humans in conducting medical research and save billions of dollars in the process? And the truth was that the robot that had replaced her was publishing papers left and right since it never slept.

If she wanted to keep her job, and maybe get Adrián re-hired, she needed to increase the aggression. Making the robots look like idiots was too soft a goal. She needed to hit the system where it really hurt.

After getting home, she calculated the decay of a magnetic field. Magnetic field strength had an inverse cube relationship with distance. The calculation was easy, but she stilled double checked it. She tried to sleep, waiting until the robot shift ended, then returned to the chemistry department's basement. She made sure to leave all metal items, her purse, and phone by the computer. The silence in the room told her there was no one around. The joints in her hands and knees ached as she stripped the red tape from the floor, and made a new perimeter closer to the NMR, then she set the cones on top of the new tape line.

***

Bárbara walked into the basement and dropped the spray bottle, spilling blue glass cleaner on the floor.

"Oh my God," she said, forcing tears down her cheeks; definitely award-winning acting.

Stuck to the magnet were John John and Mike. The robot bodies were twisted into each other like a pair of contortionists that had attempted a two-human pretzel.

"I don't know how this happened," the chemistry department chair, Dr. Markson, said. "They had been warned many times. No metal beyond the cones."

Bárbara tensed for a second, but neither of them men noticed that someone had moved the perimeter a bit closer to the NMR. Her trap was too subtle for these two bureaucrats to pick up on.

Director Rhodes nodded. "This is not good. A good number of students came in before we closed off the floor. I'm guessing the noise made them curious. It's all over social media already. Why are their faces melted like that?" He looked over to Bárbara, but she continued to cry, covering her mouth in case a smile slipped.

"A bottle of some organic solvent must have made its way over and probably shattered when they smashed into the magnet, spilling the liquid everywhere. Maybe one of them was holding it while the other cleaned," Dr. Markson said, pointing to broken glass beneath one of the robot's hanging feet. "This is going to be unimaginably expensive to fix."

"If a student had been here and ended up hurt, we'd be on our way to court already," Rhodes said.

That was all she needed to hear. Bárbara turned to leave

and surreptitiously took a picture of the two deformed robots from the door.

Once she got home, she made a meme with the picture side by side a Freddy Kruger snapshot, the main bad guy from the movie *A Nightmare on Elm Street*, then captioned her meme with "Who wore it better?" She posted the meme on a fake twitter account and tagged the school, the chemistry department, even Rhodes' personal account. Enough students were talking about it online, so no one would suspect her.

That evening, her phone pinged with an email. It was long, and full of official language stating that robots had been banned from campus until future notice. She was sure they would be back soon enough though. Many jobs depended on them.

Some science departments were concerned about how much safety awareness robots had, especially those that mentored students in a lab setting. If the robots were immune to most toxic substances could they still have enough empathy to protect human students when around said substances?

A file was also attached to the email, a job offer, giving Bárbara her a non-tenure track professor and researcher position, along with a significant amount of money from the chemistry departments' emergency fund to restart her lab. New challenges might arise in the few years before she retired, but those were problem she'd address as they arrived. She accepted the offer immediately.

Souling

Hannah Gilchrist

G ordy shielded himself against the wind as the lawyer unlocked the front door, and they stepped inside to the grand front hall as quickly as possible. Gordy's eyes immediately cut left to the shamble of boards that had been nailed up to block off the east wing. Not as bitterly cold as outside, still there poured a draft from between the boards that smelled of rank dust and claustrophobic air.

"He was afraid," Gordy said.

"Of what?" the attorney asked.

Gordy tried to imagine the house alive with his parents, with his uncle as a young man, of grandparents and cousins and aunts and other uncles and friends of the family, of children and adults and teenagers and fiancés and fiancées. He'd heard stories and was sure the house could accommodate comfortably such a battalion, though he couldn't remember seeing it for himself. For as long as he could remember, it had only been he and his uncle.

"Of Death," Gordy said. "He didn't want to die."

"But he has, and your uncle has left you a number of items to complete before you receive your sum of the inheritance."

Still cradling the briefcase against his chest, the attorney was careful to open it and extract a collection of papers stapled together, and managed to hand that paper over before clasping the briefcase without spilling out anything else. The papers contained a catalogue of to-do items and a list of what was to be donated, sold, or destroyed, and if dispersed where and how it should go. Still, there would be plenty left to Gordy even after the funeral costs were covered and the last of the medical bills paid.

"How long have you been coming to this house?" Gordy asked the attorney.

"Your uncle had my father on retainer until he retired back before you were taken in. Law school seemed a reasonable vocation, so I took up my father's client list when he could no longer serve."

"Congratulations, by the way," Gordy said. "I heard your wife is expecting."

They entered the study where Gordy found some of his uncle's port and poured them both a glass. The lawyer thanked him sheepishly, said he didn't know if it was a boy or girl yet, just that the baby appeared to be developing well in the womb. It was Gordy who steered the conversation back on course.

"I really don't like the idea of staying here any longer." He had an apartment back where he went to college, and while his professors understood that this was his only family and gave him as much time as needed to get the affairs in order, he was anxious to get back. He was not his uncle; though this was the only home he could remember and his uncle had been a caring man who had provided for him, this house was too big and too much for a single person.

"That is, unfortunately, a stipulation of the will, and as an agent of the court I am bound by the law and by your uncle's wishes to ensure that you meet that requirement in order to secure your inheritance."

Gordy downed the last of his port and poured another glass. The lawyer, he noticed, had only taken a few sips. "Jesus," he said, another drink washing down his throat, "nobody but lawyers talk like that."

The man smiled as though the stick up his ass was just slightly uncomfortable.

"I'll bring the urn tomorrow, of course. Your uncle wants it placed in his suite. I'll also check on your progress. In the meantime, if there is anything you need, don't hesitate to phone me at any time. I'll have my cell on me always. For what it's worth, Merry Christmas, sir."

"Sure thing," Gordy said as he showed the attorney to the door.

Back in the study, Gordy combined the attorney's undrunk portion with more from the bottle and sipped and rummaged the liquor cabinet for whatever else he might imbibe. He'd made doubly sure that his instructions had not that the alcohol be rationed out to some wine collector or old friend or that the stores were to be sold on eBay. "Waste not, want not," the best mantra Gordy could bring to mind, and his favorite when it came to liquor in general, and he passed the next few hours meandering through the halls of the unsealed section of the old manor and reminiscing about the Christmases long since passed.

As the night waxed on, Gordy, lost in drink and memories, buried himself so deeply in the study that he could still hear the plaintive wails of his uncle calling him to dinner, echoing through the dark and silent halls, and so engrained in the past that at these times he turned, expecting to find his uncle, catching only the fleeting shadow of movement that he attributed to the drink as the phantom sounds faded to susurrations and then to nothing, not even an echo.

The lawyer found him the next morning slumped in his uncle's chaise lounge in the study, the goblet bone dry and on its side on the floor by the chair. Only after the attorney cleared his throat for the third time did Gordy stir and peel himself out of the prone position to stagger upright.

"Get much work done," Gordy slurred, unsure if he was asking himself or confessing to the attorney, deciding only that he was still inebriated from the night before.

"I brought the urn, sir," the attorney said, displaying the metal box held in both hands.

Gordy led him from the study and up the stairs to his uncle's suite, and the box found its way to the mantle of the fireplace. Gordy, perhaps due to the draft blasting through the walls that sobered him more, decided to make a fire in the stone firebox. He pulled out logs from the abutting wood box and laid them on the hearth, and he cleaned out the ashes and spread a bit of kindling and lit a starter log he'd found in a box next to the stacks of oak and green pine. Soon the suite warmed and a healthy flame brightened the large room.

"I think I'll sleep in here tonight," Gordy said, feeling the invitation of his uncle's old room.

"I think you should, sir," the attorney agreed.

"Would you like a drink?" Gordy asked, then thought better of it, and added, "Or something to eat? I could go for some lunch."

"I really must be getting back to town, sir," the attorney said.

"It's no trouble," Gordy said, and heard the excitement in his own voice. The whispers and fleeting glances from the night before returned, Gordy now less susceptible to the rationale he'd attributed to them, and while the room was inviting, the rest of the house was decidedly cold and dark. He could not ignore what he'd seen, what he'd heard, and the drunk logic he'd used to dismiss the visitations now failed miserably in the light of day.

"Is everything okay?" the attorney asked.

The bedroom window was scarred with iron latticework that formed diamond patterns of glass and played shadows on the far wall, but the window stood where direct sunlight could never reach it, and it struck Gordy for the first time just how resistant to sunlight this house was. Every shutter drawn, every window closed, and not enough windows to provide natural light into this too-large home, as though his uncle were an enemy to the day. When the attorney left, Gordy set about the house, opening as many shutters as he could, leaving only those shut where the window was in a state of disrepair or the glass missing, the weather-stripping dry and cracked, the framework rusted or busted. Still, as he stood in the great hall in the middle of the afternoon, the house succumbed to the darkness. Gordy found his interest piqued at the sealed off portion of the manor from where the cold draft seemed to originate.

With crowbar and hammer procured from the shed in the back yard, he removed the boards that blocked the east wing arch.

The hall yawned, pitch and silent, the draft unabated, a torrent or a gust that blasted him. Had his uncle, in health, driven the nails to secure the boards against this entrance, or had the attorney helped, or had one or the other hired a local handyman for this work? Gordy was sweating, and he knew he was in better shape than his uncle and he was sure he was in better shape than the suit-pressed, bespectacled barrister who primly pimped his mannerisms as though he were the better man. Snobby bastard probably would consider getting his hands dirty a debasement.

So why then, he pondered, fetching a flashlight and checking the batteries, did his uncle so completely seal off this section of the house? Standing at the precipice again, crowbar in one hand and flashlight in the other, the draft ruffling his hair like some great yawn from a slumbering giant, Gordy remembered the sights and sounds from the night before, and he came to the realization that perhaps his uncle hadn't sealed up this portion of the house for frugality. This portion of the house held many old bedrooms, an old sitting room, attic space unconnected to the attic space of the main hall, an old kitchen which led down to the original cellar. He recalled, in fact, that what stood now as a sprawling manor home had once been just this east wing, two stories with a pitched roof. His uncle or his grandfather or someone years ago had, dipping into just a percentage of the family money, built on the addition and changed forever the hall into an estate.

He entered the wing unsure of where he'd go, deciding finally he'd just investigate room by room, mentally cataloging the items he'd see but not spending too much time in any one space. He sneezed upon entering, and continued to sneeze, his footfalls stirring up the dust that carpeted the floor. He found also that as resistant as the rest of the house seemed to be to sunlight, the east wing was utterly defiant. Even where the light tried to snake through the blinds, it was obstructed from bringing any quality of illumination to the rest of the room, so that until the beam of the flashlight swept the various and sundry furnishings and knickknacks did the claw become a candlestick or the hunkered beast become a sofa. Gordy called to mind the creeping things from the night before, and imagined again the settling house moaned to him in his uncle's voice, and the billow of a drape caught in an alien draft was the movement of some visitant to this abandoned abode. He hurried his pace, not satisfied that the house would be secure till he'd seen every room, but he was sure he didn't want to be caught in the east wing after sunset, as unreasonable fears played with his isolated imagination, suggesting danger.

In the east wing parlor, he found a book. The parlor was filled with the normal trappings found in any such room in the country, and came with its own stone fireplace not dissimilar to the one in the master suite or in the study, but the book stood out to him because of where it was placed and because of its cover, which he could see easily enough when the beam of his light fell on it. He stood at the door, hesitant to enter. The book appeared leather-bound, the cover adorned with a goat-like head with furled horns on either side, its title written in embossed gold script in a language he thought was Latin. It rested, closed, on the coffee table, as though someone had been reading it and had left it there with a place holder till they could return to it.

Despite his better judgment, his fear and his curiosity clawing from opposing sides at his intrepidness, Gordy entered the room and approached the book.

He sat on the dust-covered couch with a plop and a plume of dust and coughed then sneezed again, bent and placed the crowbar to his side, and ran his fingers over the letters.

"Mort-i-mag-o-leg-is," he sounded out. He ran the sounds

over his tongue a few more times, then said *"Mortimagolegis."*

It was a hefty tome, its gilded-edged pages like something out of an old family Bible, easily torn if not carefully handled. The first letter of each chapter was embossed in gold and twisted into a vine-entwined animal. The thin scrawls were serpents and the fat blocked letters rams—an M more resembled a bat, and a V resembled more a stag's glaring face. He tried it with one hand and found, like a family Bible, it was too heavy. He'd have to make a choice: the crowbar, the flashlight, or the book—two but not all three. He was surprised he was considering bringing the book back at all. That face on the front, goat-like but the furrowed brow, the pupil-less eyes unblinking, and the teeth in the snout more carnivorous than any goat he'd ever seen giving it a demonic appearance, suggested that any trepidation he felt about the east wing could have come directly from this source. Perhaps this was why his uncle had shut up the house, for such a book could contain nothing pure. Gordy rose, even as the front door thundered a knock that echoed through the halls, and in that second he resolved himself to take the flashlight and the crowbar and leave the book, and nearly in a sprint he hurried out of the east wing and back into the great hall as someone rapped at the knockers again.

"Coming!" he called, nearly tripping over the boards, and decided he could easily take the hammer and pound the boards back into place to reseal that section of the house again. He reached the door as another knock rolled through the halls, swung the door open, and stood bemused and on the border of fear.

No one was there.

He stepped out onto the landing to look across the expanse of the yard; dusk would arrive soon, the lengthening shadows and dimming afternoon light a portent of the night to come, but still there was just enough light to reveal he was utterly alone. The only movement came with the gentle breeze rustling the dead leaves over the dry, drab grass.

"That I scarce was sure I'd heard you," he quoted, then, "Only darkness, nothing more." He steeled himself with a great breath that fleeted as a whimpering sigh, shut the door and locked it.

"Not tonight," he said aloud, turned and took the hammer to the nails still in the boards, and in no time the east wing was again sealed. Sweaty, he longed for a shower, but he also longed for a drink, and so returned to his uncle's study where, as he flipped on the lights, a scream welled up in his throat and threatened to erupt from his mouth, and the only reason he didn't cry out was because in a great and exhaustive gasp his breath left him and he collapsed against the wall.

The *Mortimagolegis* lay unopened on the coffee table, the great demon face glaring at him.

Gordy grabbed for the wall, and his mind searched first the fantastic and then the rational for the presence of the book. His uncle's spirit, haunting the halls, must want him to read it; the book itself is possessed; whatever knocked for him at the door must be an omnipresence desiring him to read the book. Or what if…? He brought it with him, in some sort of fugue state brought on by mold or stale air from the boarded section of the house; or he'd misidentified the book's location, and it had been in the den the whole time and he'd only thought he saw it traipsing through the boarded section of the house.

Steadying his breathing, he approached the book like a wary puppy might approach a snake hole. He opened its cover and sat down carefully. He thumbed through the pages, finding incantations, ancient carvings, spells, and rituals. He found a discussion on the soul and another on the transference of energy. He found pages and pages of script written in Latin. And scattered throughout, carvings and drawings of such imagery not unlike the beast on the cover of the book. Images of orgies between man, woman, and things that were neither, mockeries of masses, blood sacrifices.

There came another knock at the door.

Gordy walked back to the front door and opened it, thinking about the images, his only thought about the visitor that no one would be there, like before. He jumped when he found a little boy on the stoop, dressed in a black suit, a red rose pinned to his lapel that matched his blood red bow tie. The boy offered a smile that unnerved Gordy, as from the yard a wind assaulted him and just above the tree line, a lightning-flashed squall-line slowly overtook the stars, punctuated by distant rolls of rumbles.

"You better get on home, little boy," Gordy said to start, but he couldn't help but notice the way the boy was looking at him, like he knew him. "Can I help you with something?" [TPW1] Rogue drops of rain splattered on his neck. There wasn't enough of a cover over the stoop to shield the little boy.

"If you give me a piece of candy," the little boy said, "I'll pray for your soul!" And he let loose a horrible, snaggle toothed laugh and turned and ran into the squall. Gordy took a few steps forward and called for the boy, but the evening and the pressing storm had consumed him and, despite the echoing laughter, would not give him back.

***

The soul, the book revealed, could not be destroyed, but it could be relocated. Gordy had nearly finished the bottle of port, but he knew his uncle had more stashed in the cabinet. He could stay drunk for a month here while he rummaged through his uncle's things.

The soul was not superfluous, and it was not mutable. One could not retain the very definition of life without the soul; no matter where or what it inhabited, it never changed. But if the book was suggesting past lives, then it did not suggest that the soul could not forget. In fact, it made the distinction that while a soul may not remember where it was before, this did not mean that the soul had changed. It had merely forgotten.

Outside, the storm had overtaken the estate. Rain pelted the roof and windows, metronomic and lightning crashed metallically and intermittently. The wind wailed and rallied against the eaves, and throaty thunder rattled the walls and windows of the home. And despite all this, Gordy could still hear the deliberate booming knocks suggesting someone stood at his door.

It was the boy, he was sure, lost in the rain and remorseful for his practical joke. And while he was sure it served the boy right for pulling a prank, he could not in good conscience leave a child out in this weather.

"Coming," he said, and opened the door, but the boy didn't stand on the stoop. This time a teenager stood there, dressed in his red bowtie that matched his red rose and his black suit. He stood bone-dry on the stoop as the storm raged around him, not even a hair out of place, though the wind tousled Gordy's hair and blades of rain stabbed at his cheeks and forehead and his left hand bracing him on the door jam.

"If you give me something to eat," the teenager said, "I'll pray for your soul."

Gordy slammed the door and locked it.

He leaned against the door, listening for the young man on the stoop, but only hearing the rain. Maybe he should have let the kid in, but why was he dressed like the little boy, and why was he not wet, and why the hell were they saying the same thing? As the book appeared, he suddenly feared the boy or the teen would appear as well, and he rushed back to the study, thankful only to find the book and the rest of the room as he left it.

***

Shortly after midnight, Gordy had quelled his fears with another two glasses of port and had retired with the book to his uncle's suite, he hoped well out of earshot of the front door. He locked the suite and started a fire and sat with the book closed, drinking and staring at the bed. He'd contemplated not bringing the book but knew his fears would overwhelm him if he left it in the study only for it to resurface here mysteriously. *No, don't think about such things[TPW2]* . He'd grabbed a few more bottles to keep him company through the rest of the long night, and there was still plenty downstairs he could retrieve once the sun came up.

So why even stay? He stared at the bed, at the spot where his uncle had died, his Cheyne-Stoke death rattle, eyes flitting, skin ashen, finger-tips purpling. This house had become a funerary for him, as dead as his only family.

His uncle praised the isolation and felt like a king when he could survey his land from horizon to horizon. So where had those goddamn kids come from? That's it, then, he thought. Too much to drink. He'd had too much; he always knew he'd had too much when the curse words flowed too easily. His uncle had always said only the ignorant cuss.

He sat down his glass and turned with a new vigor inspired by just enough alcohol and just enough mourning to the collection of boxes in the corner of the room nearest the bookcase. These had been brought down by hired hands from the lawyer (they were too dusty and had too many spider corpses and cobwebs for the lawyer himself, Gordy imagined) and were first on the list to be sorted. The first box, labeled pictures, seemed innocuous enough, so Gordy opened it and began to rummage, and nearly instantly felt his breath leave him again.

It couldn't be. Just couldn't. It was impossible, but there, in his hands, undeniable proof that conjured memories so palpable he could hear his uncle's voice again. "Gordon. In the end, it's the legacy you leave behind for others to sort through, discard, and keep."

"Why don't you have any pictures of you at my age?" Gordy had asked his uncle nearly fifteen years ago, an inquisitive child interested in learning then that his only living relative hadn't always been old. "Because I was born old," his uncle said, and he had laughed good-naturedly, and Gordy had said "No you weren't," and they had laughed together, the young and the old.

Here, framed and sepia-toned, pictures of the little boy from earlier this evening, dressed in a black suit and a bow tie and a rose, and another picture of a boy of around fifteen dressed the same, with the same furrowed brow and the same crooked smile that had illuminated his uncle's face in the firelight, that had only vanished as he gasped for breath under the watchful gaze of his nephew, his doctor, his nurse, and his lawyer. Popping the backs off, Gordy's fears were confirmed when he saw the pencil-scrawled date and name. Montague, age 10, Montague, age 15. And the date. The date! By god, the date, impossible as it was—March, 1838 and on the other—September, 1843. The dates—after a quick calculation and a double-check given how inebriated he was, suggested his uncle had been almost two-hundred years old! Impossible, Uncle Montague, and he screamed this, and because he wasn't ready for the pictures and rationalizing them with the visitors, he took a good long drink then smashed the glass into the fireplace, then opened the bottle of Pinot and took a long pull from the neck and felt his world swoon. He blinked and imagined his uncle lying in the bed, looking at him with those dead eyes, gasping for breath. What if he had seen with those eyes, Gordy thought? Those horribly lifeless, listless eyes, that should have robbed his vision and his understanding. What if he saw with those eyes? What if he was aware of his breath leaving him by startles and spurts? What if he could feel the life leaving him?

As if to answer, another knock from the door below, the sound climbing up the steps to rap on the chamber door, and Gordy thought of his loving uncle who'd provided for him and given him a good life with good instruction, and sure sometimes they butted heads like families do, but they always came around, especially when they were needed, family always came around. His uncle was coming around now, and he was needed. Gordy threw open the door and bolted down the stairs, one hand on the railing to guide him, taking the stairs by twos and threes until he was at the door and he'd tossed it open and all the sounds of the storm returned and in front of him stood not a child or a teenager but a young man, still dressed in the dark suit with the bow tie that matched the rose in his pocket.

Gordy understood so much now. He was no longer afraid for himself, but worried that his uncle had met something tragic and permanent on the other side. He smiled and held out a hand from which the young man retreated a step, but did not stop smiling.

"Uncle Montague, you should have told me. If I'd known you were in trouble… What do you need from me?"

"Give me something to eat, maybe to drink," the young man said. "And I'll pray for your soul."

Gordy understood.

"Come in," he said and turned to light the path toward the kitchen, and stumbled and caught himself and spun again, only to find he was alone in the front hall.

Gordy turned in place, searching, pleading. His uncle was in trouble and he couldn't help him if his uncle didn't ask, and that's what he was doing. Asking, right? A crash from above drew his attention up the stairs; Gordy could place it instantly. As quickly as he had descended he bounded up the stairs and rushed back into his uncle's empty suite, and found the source of the sound.

The urn had not been precariously placed on the hearth. There had been plenty of room, and it was not in danger of teetering or tottering. Still, it lay on the floor, the lid open, and Gordy approached cautiously, sure he was encroaching on his uncle's last remains. But he noticed something as he approached, and what he saw caused him to hurry across the floor and bend and pick up the urn. The hasp had snapped and the lid dangled on one hinge, but no ash had spilled because no ash filled the interior. The urn's interior was dry and clean, like it had never held a particulate or a cinder.

Gordy thought of the visitors dressed like his uncle in the pictures and asked aloud: "Where are you, Uncle Montague?"

He should have been in the urn. Just what kind of fucked up game was that lawyer playing, anyway? The lawyer. The idea of the attorney behind these shenanigans muddled Gordy's image of the uptight attorney and humanized the barrister all at once. But what could he gain, tormenting the heir like this? Gordy got the bright idea to ask him himself. He set the urn down and picked up the portable and dialed but received no other sound for several seconds, and then a gasp of a breath, and then another, like a rattle, like snoring almost, and then nothing. And just as he was about to speak, another great gasp for air, a few snores, and settling, shallower, shallower, till nothing.

"Uncle?" his voice shook as he spoke into the phone. "Uncle Monty?"

The voice that answered was dry and raspy and filled with those struggling sounds, the gurgling, choking, gasping sounds of a body trying to hang on to...

"Give me something to eat and I'll pray for your soul."

Gordy hung up the phone.

His keys he found downstairs in the study after he tied his shoes, and he remembered that upon meeting the attorney, he had pulled around and parked in the garage.

Flicking on the garage light, he saw his Prius, and saw his uncle's old Cadillac, and saw the young man still in his suit standing in front of the driver's side door of the Prius. Gordy clenched the keys in his sweaty palms and struggled to find his own breath. When he spoke, his own voice rattled.

"You want me safe, Uncle. You want me safe. You wanted to pray for my soul."

The young man no longer smiled. "It's too late for that."

And then he lunged and Gordy tried to scream, but he only saw black.

***

186

The lawyer hovered over him, examining him, and seemed to be waiting patiently for Gordy's eyes to open. He helped Gordy to his feet and led him back into the kitchen out of the garage, and poured a glass of water with three ice cubes and let Gordy drink it down and fixed him another.

"Am I safe to assume it worked, sir?" the attorney asked.

"Just cold enough," Gordy said. His voice different. Older. Raspier. "Three ice cubes."

"That is how you've always taken it. That is how my father said you took it."

To this Gordy let out a chuckle, and closed his eyes to the memories fresh to his mind. These were Montague's memories, from Montague's perspective. He downed the last of the water and winced a bit, then began snapping his fingers. Anticipating this, the attorney fished through the drawers till he produced a bottle of aspirin and dumped several into Gordy's hands.

"Jesus," he said, and washed the aspirin down with a fresh cold glass offered by the lawyer, "I didn't want him to drink so much."

"And what now, sir?" the lawyer asked, returning the bottle to the drawer. "Father said you might look for an orphan."

"No, no, too soon," the other said, waving his hands. "Much too soon for that, old chap. We'll find one when the time is right, when we are very old and I have used up this body. And I will love the little street urchin. Love him without boundaries, like he was my own son. He'll never suspect anything else, as long as I love him, once I'm old. Now is the time for revelry, and … do you know what you're having?"

"We are going to the doctor tomorrow, sir."

"Son or daughter," he said with a shrug, "just make sure that the family practice carries on. I can't go to just any lawyer with this."

The two men laughed. Gordy clapped his arms [TPW3] around the attorney and hugged his shoulders and said, "I'm famished!" like it was an epiphany and the attorney said that there was a diner down the road—Melinda's, he believed the name was—and Gordy asked if she was still alive, and the attorney shook his head.

"No sir, you are remembering her grandmother. It seems we have a lot to catch you up on."

"We have time," the old soul said. "We have an eternity."

Nostalgia

Jacob Steven Mohr

Growing up, my mother kept a garden of hands. Pale grasping hands on slender stalk wrists, reaching up from the soil in our backyard. The hands were not of a size; no two were alike at all. Some were scarred, or bore tattoos. Some were missing fingers. Some were smooth and whole. But they all stuck in the ground the same way, emerging where the elbow would bend on a normal arm. Palms open, they followed the sun, and their fists shut tight when night fell.

Then we had to move away from that house. When people came to look the property over, the garden of hands was already gone and paved over smooth. Not a speck of soil was out of place; no trace remained that our strange crop had ever grown there. I don't know what became of the hands. My mother, silent and dark and full of secrets, never spoke of them again. But I'm grown now and my thoughts will often fly back to that strange garden of my youth, to my mother's secret harvest of wrists and fingers.

And when people pass on the street, I watch what extends from their sleeves. And I wonder.

Melpomene's Garden

Curtis Harrell

The horse's eye was wide with terror. Lauren knelt with one knee pressing the horse's heaving neck into the mud while the veterinarian, with her strong, sure fingers, probed along the horse's jaw up to its trachea.

"Hold her still," the vet admonished sternly. "You've got to keep her from hurting herself."

Lauren exerted more pressure on the horse's neck, until the frantic animal could no longer thrash. She knew only the eyes of her grandfather's horses, all liquid brown and long-lashed as the animals nuzzled sugar from her flat palm. This eye, though brown, was ringed with panicked white, and Lauren was frightened. She turned her head and brushed sandy mud from the great muscle that swelled above the horse's foreleg. She smoothed the short, silky coat so she would not have to see.

"That's right, calm her down," the vet said, quiet now, her voice soothing. "I think this old girl only had a scare."

Lauren looked up from the frightened beast, across a hundred yards of mud where other horses either struggled to extract themselves or lay motionless. In places, only legs and

190

hooves protruded above the silt. She realized that, only an hour before, this must have been a grassy meadow. Now it was an expanse of mud. A wide freshet, red, the color of clay, streamed down the middle, shallow enough to wade. She looked behind her, at the school van, its doors flung open, ten feet from where the road disappeared beneath the shining silt. An hour before, she had been on a field trip with her journalism class to observe the news teams covering the flood. Now they were all volunteers.

"This isn't the main deluge," Mr. Harris, her journalism teacher, shouted at his students, waving them to circle him. "This is just a horse pond that gave way on the side of that hill."

Lauren stayed with the frightened mare even though the vet had moved on to another animal. She stroked the wide, muscular neck, and, under her touch, the horse calmed, the eye half-closed.

"Find out the topography," Mr. Harris yelled, gesticulating at the countryside. "Interview any of these locals to get a description of the pond before it came down. Remember what the first news crew said about soil saturation this morning. This pond came down from the dam side being saturated with all the rain, not from the pressure of the current. Find out how big the pond was. It must have been a pretty good size. See if you can find out in surface acres. Find out where the horse barn used to be. Estimate distances."

Lauren sat down hard in the mud when the chestnut mare suddenly struggled to her feet; she scrambled backward, expecting the horse to bolt. But the mare took a shaky step toward her and nuzzled her long hair. When she rose to join Mr. Harris, the mare nipped at her shoulder.

"See if you can find the owner of the horses," Mr. Harris

continued. "Get a head count. See how many animals were killed, how many are going to have to be destroyed."

When two boys from her class ran past, the horse nudged its long head under Lauren's arm until she held it across its withers. The mare kept its head bent to nuzzle at Lauren's other hand.

"If you aren't trying to get an interview, come with me in the van. We're going to drive back up the road to that store and phone in the story to the paper. We've scooped the big boys on this one. We got lucky."

Mr. Harris jogged across the mud toward the van, a broad smile across his face. Lauren was giving the horse a final stroke when a terrified whinny from across the field spooked the mare, and Lauren was jerked off the ground. She fell at the mare's feet, and the horse shied away, its pupil dilated with panic again. Mr. Harris was already starting the van motor. Lauren looked back across the mud to see the vet struggling with a huge black stallion, huge even buried to its flanks in the silt. She struggled to her feet and raced to where the giant horse labored to free itself.

"Hold his head still," the vet commanded.

Lauren straddled the stallion's withers, her feet barely touching the ground even though the mud was to his shoulders. She leaned forward and took the massive neck in both arms, her face buried in his mane. The stallion thrashed and violently shook his head so that her face banged the bony point between his ears. She felt her lip fatten, and her chin grew raw from the friction of his mane. She hugged the great head as tightly as she could, pressing her cheek against one silken ear.

"Good," the vet panted as she tried to grasp his lower lip, "hold him tight."

The stallion continued to pitch his head from side to side, but Lauren held on like death. She could feel the supple spine and engorged muscles working between her thighs where she hugged him with her legs. She could feel each ragged whinny in the hollow of her chest, vibrating through the air in her own lungs. She held him until he began to tire, and the vet, loosening Lauren's grip from around his neck, slid her hands down over the stallion's eyes. The huge horse quieted, and his long lashes tickled her cupped palms as he blinked. The vet skinned off her windbreaker and draped it over his forelock.

"This will make a better blinder."

The stallion relaxed in Lauren's grasp, and the huge jaw sank until his nostrils flared in the soft mud. Now it was Lauren who struggled to move the stallion. She cradled his head with both arms wrapped around his neck, her cheek resting on the windbreaker covering his eyes. Her back began to ache from leaning forward, holding the weight of the stallion's long head. She straddled him stiff-legged, and the back of her knees tightened and went numb. But the vet had rounded up a few men, and they began to dig out the animal with shovels, garden trowels, their bare hands, anything available. One man scraped back the silt with a board from the horse barn, and he was the first to unearth the stallion's left hock. When blood began to ooze up through the sotted soil, he discarded his board and dug with his hands too.

"Be careful," the vet warned Lauren, "when he starts feeling like he can get loose from the mud, he might start thrashing again."

But the stallion let his head remain limp in Lauren's aching arms. She cradled his throat in the crook of her left arm, and, when it began to quiver with fatigue, she switched to her right arm. With her free hand, she stroked the huge beast, starting with his muddy nose, and then dropped her hand under his chin to smooth the loose skin there.

"Hey, doc," the man who discarded the board said, "come take a look at this."

The vet disappeared from Lauren's view, and, because of her struggle to hold the stallion, she could not turn to see what the vet studied. There was a long silence. Then Lauren heard a wet slap across the stallion's flank, but the horse remained limp in her arms. Lauren didn't feel the stallion so much as flinch.

"Okay, go ahead and do it," the vet said after another silence.

Lauren felt the vet's hand on her shoulder.

"C'mon, honey. Lay him down."

She suddenly realized what decision had been made, and she hugged the stallion with both arms, pressed her cheek into his long mane.

"C'mon, darlin', we can't help him any more."

Lauren hugged the huge head even tighter, felt one tear burn as it rolled down her cheek. A rough hand grabbed her by the back of her belt and lifted her from the stallion. The horse's head dropped, muzzle-first into the soft mud, and she saw the black barrel of a rifle swing up to the place where she had pressed her face against the stallion's silky ear. Struggling against the force that dragged her from the horse, she cried out, and, at the sound of her voice, the black stallion, though blinded, raised its head from the silt and cocked its ears. Lauren spun to loose herself, and sprawled flat in the slick silt. Before she could turn back to the stallion, a rifle crack split the air, the sharp concussion pressed her eardrums, the echo rang in her head. She scrabbled to her feet, without looking back, and ran through the shallow freshet, across the mud and into the shade of the trees. She ran into the forest, stumbling and swatting branches as they clawed at her face, and, finally, collapsed at the edge of a small glen, because the running and the sobbing would not let her breathe.

When the jerking spasms of her sobbing subsided, and the canopied green of the glen sharpened out of blur when she blotted away her tears with her shirttail, she became aware of a house at the other end of the clearing. Lauren hoped there was a telephone there, so she could call home, have her mother come to pick her up. There must be a road, she reasoned, on the other side of the house, and she was relieved. She did not want to have to cross the washout again. Picking herself up from the moss and moldy leaves, she waded through the waist-high ferns to the door of the house, which was open.

"Hello," Lauren called into the house.

The house was tidy and well-kept for a structure that seemed to have sprouted, like the ferns, from the mossy floor of the glen. Although she stood before the front door on a wide flagstone at the bottom of the small porch's two stone steps, she could see no path that led here. She turned in a circle and saw that even the ferns she had trampled to get here had sprung back, giving no indication of her passing. Lush vegetation grew right up to the house's foundation, and the house rose two stories up into the shady green of the trees' canopy. The house seemed to be of Victorian design; the porch railings, the shutters, and the eaves, high in the green shadows, were webbed with fancy scrollwork.

"Hello, anybody home?" Lauren called again through the open door.

But still there was no response. Maybe, she thought, whoever lived here had heard the commotion of the flood and had gone to help out. Lauren strained her ears to listen for any sound from the house, but her head still rang from the rifle's blast. She climbed the steps and walked through the door, stopping just past the threshold. She was in a long hall that went to the back of the house. At the hall's other end, through the open rectangle of the back door, she could see more abundant green, and flowers, a lavish confusion of color and shadow. To Lauren's right, a doorway led into a wallpapered room. Still straining to listen, she ventured inside, immediately noticing the odd arrangement of the furniture: an overstuffed sofa and chairs, a coffee table with carved legs and marquetted top, an imposing armoire, all pushed to the center of the room and arranged there. The perimeter of the room was bare. No furniture was against the papered walls. Lauren, in her search for a telephone, circumnavigated the room at its outside edge, ending back at the doorway. Although she had seen no phone in her tour of the room, she had noticed, as she had circled and her eyes grew accustomed to the muted light from the draped window, that the flowered wallpaper was worn at shoulder height, all the way around the room, faded in a line a few inches high. She turned to examine the wall beside the doorway, and she could see that the wallpaper, where there was no pattern, was beginning to show white. Where the line crossed over a printed flower, the design paled. She stepped back into the hallway, and, although the hall was painted, she could detect the worn line where it had dulled the enamel's gloss.

"Do you have a telephone I could use?" Lauren called up the stairway.

The strange house was silent. She continued down the hallway, to the next open door, on her left, beneath the carved staircase. In this room, the peculiar worn place was strikingly clear. The wallpaper was a floral design, chrysanthemum and peony blossoms raised in faux velvet on a ribbed satin field. Where the line circled the room at shoulder height, the nappy raised blooms had been worn as flat as the satin background, and as shiny. Again, no furniture encumbered the walls, and, in the center of the room, on carved marble pedestals, gathered the mute busts of men and women, mingling as at a disembodied dinner party. Lauren thought she recognized some of the statues. Was that Hamlet proffering Yorick's skull? Was the young girl who stared wistfully out of the half-draped window Anne Frank? Lauren walked into the frozen crowd and put her own face near the cold, marble ones. Each bust was dustless, immaculate. Each glowed with a filmy patina, as though polished by a person's palm.

From upstairs, there came a voice — a woman's voice — clear, coquettish, rhythmic, as if she were singing, or reciting. Lauren scampered back into the hallway, out from under the staircase, and craned her head up to glimpse a young woman descending the stairs. She wore a long gown, and, instead of holding the rail, she ran her fingers lightly across the wall at shoulder height. Lauren tried to speak, but she panicked, caught in this woman's house like a burglar. The woman dismounted the staircase and ran her hand along the wall until reached the open front door. She stopped and reached out for the opposite wall, placing her fingers on the worn spot, and then she turned and faced Lauren.

"I'm sorry," Lauren blurted, "I'm trying to find a telephone. I didn't know that anyone was home. The door was open..."

The young woman, her eyes closed, her pretty mouth downturned in an expression of exquisite sadness, made no response to this confession. Instead, she turned and entered the first room Lauren had explored. As Lauren took a hesitant step down the hall, to follow her, she heard the woman's voice, clear and melodious, resonate out into the hallway.

"The dying nightingale will cry tonight, its mournful song will echo through the glen. Then day will shaft its warmth down through the leaves, and silence her, her song lost like the night."

Lauren stepped into the doorway and watched the woman circle the room, her slender fingers gliding along the wall. Although the woman was silent now, the dying utterance of her words seemed to hover in the air, a sound like a wet fingertip circling the rim of a crystal goblet. The woman brushed past her as she returned to trace her way down the hallway, and her long gown, as it billowed and slid past Lauren's fisted hands, was as soft as the stallion's ears. She felt a deep pity welling within her, as though the satiny touch of the gown had irritated a tender part of her soul, a part that yearned for things lost.

"From marble, I will fashion ornate vessels, to hold her vanished song, its liquid shape. And when the night returns, but she is gone, then I can drink from her exquisite sadness."

The alluring voice, with its crystal, lingering afternote, flowed out from the bust room, and Lauren moved toward it with delicious slowness, down the hallway, as though she pressed through the delicate mass of a thousand hanging silken scarves.

"But can that quaff, so bittersweet, replace my nightingale, her quickened, feathered heart? No, no, this potion cannot sate my thirst. My vessel empties and my mouth is dry."

Lauren watched the young woman kneel in the center of the statues, her gown spread around her in soft heaps and folds. She caressed a sculpture which Lauren had not noticed before, a green marble carving of a stallion rearing, mane flying, hooves clawing.

"My child, is it the nightingale I miss? Is it her absence that has saddened me? Or is it me I suffer for, alone, bereft, and silent in the empty night?"

The woman turned her face to Lauren and opened her cataracted eyes. In a single, fluid motion, she rose through the mute assemblage, her arms outstretched, and cradled Lauren's face in her soft hands.

"The things we love and lose live on in us. Forget yourself, and you can give them life."

The woman took Lauren's hand and led her to the back door. There was no road, as she had expected, but a riotous garden. The sun's rays slanted steeply through the green canopy as evening deepened, and she descended the steps into the middle of the crimsons and mauves, the feathery golden petals of sunflowers and susans. Lauren looked back over her shoulder, but the doorway was empty. From somewhere in the house, she heard the melodious voice, its crystalline echo. Lauren moved among the nodding blossoms as though she were wading through transparent, tingling water, the ghost of a deluge. She became aware of the rhythmic plod of her heart, and then sound resonated outside of her, faster, a distant gallop. The muffled beat of hooves on moss grew closer, filled up her chest. From the other side of a cloud of honeysuckle, a black stallion shouldered through the sweet-tongued blooms and snorted, his long-lashed eye half-closed and liquid brown. In the midst of the colourful rabble of flowers and the heady, perfumed air, he lowered his head to let Lauren stroke his porcelain horn.

About the Authors

Matthew **Anthony Allair** is an independent filmmaker, screen writer and prose writer. He is the creator and editor-in-chief of *The X-Files Lexicon*, a reference based site about the 90s FOX television series. Through this association, he has worked for 20th Century Fox and Trailer Park, and his website has gained the attention of significant media personalities. He had made numerous appearances on podcasts, and a guest appearance on the bay area TV horror host show, *Creature Features*. He has been an entertainment writer for *Den Of Geek* and *Celeb Magazine*. He is also an independent artist, musician and song writer. He has several short form film projects in development for his independent company *Lotus Light Productions*. He temporarily lives in Petaluma , CA with his cat, Peter. He is the son of musician John Allair.

N. A. Battaglia is a horror writer haunting upstate New York with his wife, baby boy, and dog. His nonfiction work has appeared in the ABA, NYSBA, and several peer-reviewed journals, while his fiction has recently appeared in the horror anthology *Every Dark Thing*. He has several other forthcoming publications in at least two other horror anthologies. You can follow him on Twitter "Nick Writes Law and Horror" @nickthelawyerNY or on his website www.NABattaglia.com.

Much of **Evan Baughfman's** writing success has been as a playwright, his original plays finding homes in theaters worldwide. A number of his scripts are published through Heuer Publishing, YouthPLAYS, Next Stage Press, and Drama Notebook. A resident of Southern California, Evan is a theater company member with Force of Nature Productions.

Evan has also found success writing horror fiction, his work found most recently in anthologies by No Bad Books Press, 4 Horsemen Publications, and Black Hare Press. Evan's first short story collection, *The Emaciated Man and Other Terrifying Tales from Poe Middle School,* is published through Thurston Howl Publications. His spooky novella, *Vanishing of the 7th Grade,* will be released by D&T Publishing in 2022. More information is available at amazon.com/author/evanbaughfman.

K. D. Bowers is a writer who reigns in Western Pennsylvania. He found the love of writing at an early age from reading the greats like Ray Bradbury and Roald Dahl. He is currently attending CCAC and plans to go to the University of Pittsburgh in the next few years. His latest piece of fiction can be found in *Scare Street's Night Terrors* volume 9. When he is not writing, you will find him playing in his band Ladylike, painting in acrylic, and cooking.

Arasibo Campeche is originally from Puerto Rico and has a Ph.D. in Biochemistry and Biophysics. He writes science fiction, fantasy, and horror that's often inspired by scientific principles. His work has appeared in *Latinx Screams, Daily*

Science Fiction, Tales to Terrify ,Weirdbook #41, *Helios Quarterly Magazine,* among other places. Follow him on Twitter @ArasiboC.

Koji A. Dae is a queer American writer living in Bulgaria with her husband and two children. She writes dark stories and poetry that focus on the horror of motherhood and the possibility of family. She has work published in Daily Science Fiction, Zooscape, and Bards & Sages Quarterly, among others. When not writing, she's camping, hiking, dancing, or dreaming of these things. You can find out more about her at kojiadae.ink.

Hannah Gilchrist self isolates with a good cup of coffee and her cats, but when she does venture out, it is to observe the world and see how deranged it has become. Otherwise, she's an avid reader who owns a computer, but no TV or phone.

Dale Hankins is a late bloomer, publishing his first story at the tender age of 70. He has always been a writer. In addition to writing for newspapers, he spent decades writing proposals, educational materials, and research papers for multinational businesses. He wrote to live.

On the morning of 9/11, 2001 surgeons removed Dale's cancerous kidney. The operation was a complete success, but the trauma awakened Dale's mental illness. He has been hospitalized multiple times, undergone dozens of ECT treatments and been prescribed the entire gamut of psychotropic medications. He still struggles but he has learned one valuable lesson – he must write to survive.

J.D. Harlock is a Lebanese Palestinian Syrian writer based in Beirut. His short stories have been featured in The Deadlands, Sciencefictionary, Defenestration, Wyldblood Press, Antihumanist, and the Decoded Pride Anthology, his poetry has been featured in Penumbric, Future Fire, Frozen Wavelets, Mobius and Black Cat Magazine, and his articles/reviews have been featured NewMyths.com Mermaids Monthly, Interstellar Flight Press, Blood Knife and on the SFWA Blog.

You can find him on Twitter and Instagram @JD_Harlock.

Curtis Harrell writes in northwest Arkansas where he also busks with the banjo and sometimes leads tours through a cave in the summer. He has recently had short fiction, poetry, and plays published in *The Cave Region Review, The Healing Muse, Allegro Poetry Magazine, Fleas on the Dog,* and *riprap journal,* where one of his poems was nominated for inclusion in the *Pushcart Anthology.*

Priscilla Kint (she/her) is a Dutch author of short stories and Young Adult fiction. After taking part in the Creative Writing minor at Maastricht University, she successfully completed the MA Creative Writing at Bath Spa University in 2018. She's had work published by Luna Station Quarterly and occasionally dabbles in spoken word poetry. Her stories usually involve a hint of magic, a sense of danger, and confused but headstrong teenagers. Priscilla currently lives in the Netherlands, where she works as a cybersecurity analyst during the day and writes on her next novel at night. You can find her on Twitter: @priscillareads.

Erik McHatton's passion for horror literature began in grade school and can be credited to an early fascination with the "Terrific Triples" horror collections of Helen Hoke. In those books, he plumbed the depraved depths of Poe, Lovecraft, Dunsany, Bloch, Bradbury and more and was forever after put under the spell of those masters. These days he describes himself as a loving father, a tolerable husband, an adequate pet owner.

Jacob Steven Mohr was *not* raised by wolves. Feral children are capable of many things, but weaving wild words into flesh and fantasy isn't one of them. Lucky us. If it were, we'd all be speaking Wolf. Mohr's work has previously appeared in *Night Terrors*, *All Dark Places 3*, and *Liquid Imagination*, as well as on the stage of the Browncoat Theater in Wilmington, NC. He lives in Columbus, Ohio.

Darren Todd is a freelance book editor for Evolved Publications, and his short fiction has appeared in more than thirty publications over the years. He has had four plays and a feature-length film produced and a non-fiction book published.

While some of his works fall under the literary umbrella, he often returns to the speculative and horror genres. His style and reading preferences tend toward the psychological, as he enjoys stories that linger in the imagination long after he's closed the book on them.

He lives in Asheville, North Carolina with his son and girlfriend. See what he's up to darrentodd.net.

Rachel Unger thinks that now is an excellent time for us all to be kind to each other. Yes, really. She spends her days excavating stories from the dirt, staring down a microscope, and daydreaming about her next bike ride. You can find her online at www.fictionbuffet.com.

Made in the USA
Las Vegas, NV
29 May 2022

49513964R00132